Twin Screw

Two Means of Propulsion

By Terry Lee LeMaster

PublishAmerica
Baltimore

First printing

ISBN: 1-4137-0147-6
PUBLISHED BY PUBLISHAMERICA, LLLP
www.publishamerica.com
Baltimore

Printed in the United States of America

Acknowledgments

I would like to give special thanks to my oldest son, Troy LeMaster, and to my wife, Jean LeMaster, for their hard work and effort in editing my writing. Without their effort, the proper words and phrases that accent the reality of this story would not be the same. Thanks to Derrick LeMaster, my youngest son, for his special talent as an artist creating the pictures. And thanks to my sister, Rena Sue LeMaster, for giving me a computer to write with.

Jerry L. LeMaster

3 - 25 - 06

TABLE OF CONTENTS

1963
THE UNWRITTEN BOOK FOR BEGINNERS

CHAPTER ONE

A deadly quiet filled the house; Shylo James Desmond leaned back in his desk chair and listened. The high-pitched squeal of his little brother, Cannon James Desmond, and the loud scream of Joyce Marie Desmond, their mother, broke the stillness. Joyce was upset at the nine-year-old Cannon for his tracking mud across her kitchen floor. Meanwhile, Cannon was counteracting her yell of discipline with a noise of his own. Shylo went to watch the show.

Joyce, who had lost the screaming contest, grabbed Shylo by the arm as he entered the kitchen.

"Do you know where my fly swat is? I'm going to teach that child to raise his voice at me."

Thirteen-year-old Shylo was taken by surprise and could only shake his head no. Joyce let go of his arm and continued her search for the fly swat. The surprised look of fear slowly left Shylo's face and was replaced with a smile.

"Mom, I know where some really good switches are. There is a bush in the backyard with little pointed things on the branches that will draw blood when they strike the skin."

Joyce stopped, put her hands on her hips and gave Shylo a long, worried look. "I don't want to kill him!"

"No! No! Mom, it's not like the thorns on a rose bush. These thorns aren't nearly that big or sharp."

Shylo, with a great matter of urgency, went to the backyard. He knew exactly where the bush was located and how to retrieve a goodly branch. He eyed the subject, whose long, thin branches looked different from the other shrubs. The branches had the texture of an aspen tree, and the dull, pointed thorns of fat little spikes. Shylo broke a branch off and then proceeded back inside the house. Smiling and carrying the limb like a great prize, he entered the kitchen.

Joyce walked up and took the stick from Shylo's hand. "I don't think we'll need this now. But I tell you what, we'll keep it for future use."

Shylo looked at Cannon, who was sitting at the table as if nothing had happened, and then back at the switch. A look of deep concern overtook Shylo as he realized his mistake; secretly he said to himself that he wasn't going to wear shorts for a while.

It was the beginning of May, and the warmth of summer had since overtaken the Tarheel country of North Carolina. Summer vacation was just around the corner. Pine trees looked the same as ever, but all other vegetation had turned from brown to green. Shylo and Cannon were getting up earlier so they could hurry and finish the final days of school. The dog days of winter were done, and a new lifestyle was on the horizon. The mornings were always an episode of hurry up and wait; hurry to get all morning things done and be out front, waiting for the school bus before eight o'clock a.m. The bus would generally run between eight and seven minutes after eight. The driver would stop at the designated area and open the door. If you were not there, or on a visible dead run to get there, he would shut the door and leave with no problem. The bus would stop at the grade school long enough to let those students out, and then continue to its final destination, the high school. The temperature and the morning light held the promise of a very enjoyable day.

Shylo and Cannon watched the large, dark yellow passenger vehicle coming to get them. With the sounds of a very large object that was falling apart, the bus rolled to a stop and the two doors popped open. Because Shylo was four years older, and bigger, Cannon always waited while he boarded the bus first. In any other public place, Shylo was Cannon's friend and comrade. But as the order of life is, Shylo ignored him at school and on the bus to the point that he didn't even exist. Shylo went to join his two best friends, Sharon and Charles, who always reserved a seat for him. Sharon Allred and Charles Lee Deadman, both boys, were in the same class with Shylo.

CHAPTER TWO

The same teacher taught that grade all day long; only high school had different teachers for each subject. If Sharon and Charles had lived in a more populated area, they could have been referred to as being from the west side. But they lived on small farms and were only guilty of doing whatever it took to look and be street smart. It's kind of hard to be street smart on a dirt road. Sharon and Charles were discussing what had happened the day before. Unknown to the rest of the students, even Shylo, the teacher, Miss Beasley LeMon, had found them in the back of the classroom during recess, looking at x-rated magazines. As a general rule, boys are sent to the principal for disciplinary action, but in this case the teacher escorted the boys and carried the evidence in hand. The quiet attitude of all parties concerned had been a sight to behold at this assembly, to say the least. A meeting of the minds took place.

Sharon spoke, "I didn't think old lady Beasley would ever shut her mouth. I just knew any minute she was gonna choke to death on what she was trying to say."

Charles agreed with Sharon and noted, "I wonder if that old lady has ever looked at her naked body in the mirror—that must be a horrible sight for a person that old."

Shylo grinned and said, "Yeah." Shylo didn't know his own implication in the affair, and Sharon and Charles were shrewdly avoiding the whole story of what had happened. The magazines had originally come from France, brought home by Sharon's older brother, Jonathan Allred, who was in the

Army. Sharon had seized the opportunity to steal the magazines while his brother was on tour.

When the principal, Dean Higgins, asked where the magazines came from, Sharon said, "Shylo sold them to me."

After many moments of silent looks and much reasoning by the principal, he asked, "What do you think I should do about it?"

Definitely a "do not answer" question. The two boys were sent back to the classroom, while the good Mr. Dean and old lady Beasley discussed the situation. The outcome of this debate was what worried Sharon and Charles. Any form of punishment was imaginable, though it was the next day already and nothing had happened by the end of the day before.

Shylo said, "I never heard of anyone being escorted to the principal's office. I think you two have got a big-time problem."

The bus came to a stop in front of the school, and the grade school students disembarked and walked inside the building. The day proceeded as normal for Shylo's class of thirty-six students. In fact, it was so normal that by study period, when the day was three-fourths gone, Shylo had totally forgotten about Sharon's and Charles' big problem.

The stillness broke as Miss Beasley yelled, "Shylo!"

Shylo immediately looked up from his paper and answered the teacher, "Yes, ma'am."

She continued yelling with a deep, Southern Tarheel accent, "Stand up."

He stood up and remained looking back for what seemed to be a short eternity. Finally, she continued to talk without the deep, high-pitched yell. "Do you know that someday your old man is going to wake up and find out that you ain't worth the gunpowder it would take to blow your head off?"

Shylo, too afraid to speak, and knowing better than to say anything, lowered his head but kept his eyes on the teacher. She slowly returned to reading to herself. After a few moments, Shylo sat back down. Nothing was said or done to Sharon or Charles, and the rest of the day went by without incident. Shylo never found out why he had been yelled at.

CHAPTER THREE

The last day of school came and went, and the long-awaited summer vacation finally arrived. No more getting up early, going to bed early, making sure you had clean clothes or any of the other easily forgotten routines of school days. Now the day consisted of a cold cereal breakfast and nothing to do until evening television. The first two days were great, but each day after that would slowly continue to go downhill.

One week of this fun and entertainment went by. It was late afternoon, and Shylo sat on the couch, watching his mother who was frantically carrying stuff out the front door. Shylo's father, Corey James Desmond, or Jim, had been gone for five weeks. Jim drove a truck for Baker Moving and Storage, a small business whose prime carrier was Red Horse Van Lines. He was not an owner operator, but drove long-distance trips. His trips out of town that were honestly supposed to be a week would turn into weeks. His last trip from Fayetteville, North Carolina, to Springfield, Illinois, then to Kansas City, Missouri, and back to North Carolina—a one-week schedule—turned into five unforeseen weeks with pickups and drop-offs in Texas and California.

Shylo knew what his mother was doing. She was kicking Jim out again. She knew Jim was coming home, and when he got there he would find all his clothes neatly stacked in the driveway. He even had a moving truck to take it away. He had no place to take it, but that was beside the point.

Joyce sat on the couch to rest. Shylo thought she was going to say something, but she just sat there, looking down at her folded arms. Finally, she spoke. "It look's like we will have to do something."

Shylo asked, "What?"

Joyce unfolded her arms and replied, "Finish dinner." She left the room, and Shylo didn't pursue the matter anymore.

Two hours later the unmistakable sound of air brakes came through the screen door. The soiled International tractor, with no sleeper, pulling a twelve feet high and thirty feet long drop frame trailer came to a stop in front of the house. Cannon was the first one to go through the door at a fast run. Shylo followed; both boys were anxious to see their father. Joyce came out of the door rather slowly and stood on the porch, looking in the direction of her boys.

A tall, thin man with a thick head of hair, wearing grey pants and a white shirt, got out of the truck and awaited the inevitable collision with his two sons.

Joyce watched the boys hug their father, for a little, and then yelled across the lawn, "You can take your garbage and get off my property! Now!"

Jim replied, "Honey, that's not fair!"

Joyce yelled back a little louder, "Fair? Fair? Is it fair you're gone for five weeks and don't even give me a call?"

He answered, "I tried calling last week, but I never could get through on our party line."

Joyce retaliated, "Once. Once you tried calling! There are thirty-five days in five weeks, and a million onces in every day. Apparently, calling me rates about one in thirty-five million on a list of things you want to do!"

Joyce, the prosecuting attorney, paused to give Jim, the defense attorney, the opportunity of rebuttal. Jim remained silent for the moment, knowing that this was his best defense. Her voice weakened ever so slightly, and the defense knew he was winning the case.

"Your call wouldn't have made any difference! You don't just leave for weeks on end and expect everything to be hunky-dory when you get back.

Shylo and Cannon could tell their mother was cracking. Jim spoke out, submitting his best defense, bribery. "I have a suitcase full of gifts and souvenirs."

A peaceful calm overtook the jury. Jim gave Shylo a padlock key and sent him to the back of the trailer to recover the suitcase. Then the four people adjourned into the house to go through the booty in the traveling bag.

Jim watched as Shylo carried the large suitcase into the house. He thought, *I wonder if Shylo would be interested in working for me again this summer?* He remembered last summer, and it sure was a lot easier to get back in the

14

house when he was with him. And to top that off, he was now big enough to earn his keep. He would give him the going rate to load or unload—a dollar twenty-five an hour. This was an enormous increase from last year's dollar a day. Like a lot of other industry, the real busy season for moving is from the day school lets out until the day school starts. People don't like to take their children out of school to move.

cHapTer four

Five days later, Jim and Shylo left Fayetteville before daybreak with half a trailer full for Atlanta, Georgia. A little less than four hundred miles away, it was a very easy day's drive. Arriving early to take care of business was always a good idea before delivery.

Shylo watched Jim go through the gears. He knew how the clutch and gearshift operated, but was confused on how the little red button near the top of the shifting lever worked. He asked his dad, who enjoyed explaining the entire process.

"Really, it's very simple. The transmission is a regular five-speed box, and the rear end has a high and low that is operated by the red button. Push the button down—that's low—and then pull the button up for high. But the button is electric and will not operate until you let up and push back down on the fuel pedal. For example, we're in fourth high, and the next lowest gear is fourth low."

He pushed the button in, let up and pushed down on the fuel pedal. The truck went down a gear.

"Our next highest gear is back to fourth high." He pulled the button up, then let up and pushed down on the gas pedal again. The truck changed gears.

"Now, our next gear up is fifth low." He let off the fuel, put the gearshift in fifth, and just before pressing down on the pedal, he pushed the red button in.

"But as you can tell, this gear is too high." He pointed at the tachometer needle that was in the red, then pulled the button up, let off the gas, double clutched back to fourth, pushed back on the gas, and the needle on the tachometer returned to the green zone.

"See, my man, there's nothing to it. After you do that for so long it becomes second nature, and the only time you'll use the clutch is when you come to a stop."

Shylo grinned anxiously. He had driven before in Jim's lap, but he knew this year he would be driving on his own.

Three days later the Atlanta shipment was delivered, and the next day a full load of almost twenty thousand pounds was onboard for Denver, Colorado, over fourteen hundred miles away. The basic rule of measurement in the moving business is one room has a thousand pounds, and two men can load a thousand pounds an hour, or unload a thousand pounds in forty-five minutes, not counting flights of stairs or long carries.

Jim had hired three experienced men to assist with the large shipment, but the day had still been long and hard. Shylo's education in the art of handling furniture was increased by the three Georgia boys, who took the time to explain the ethics of how and why.

He was taught how to diaper a chair with a furniture pad and make sure the legs were full; how to high-low a chest of drawers to carry it; and why to start loading each tier with the hardest-to-load items first so you can fill up all the space in that tier. You fill space, you don't load furniture; although, you would never admit that to a customer. And the number one rule in loading: If possible, load the couch first. Put the feet to the wall and the back to the load.

This work was all a fact in the past, and the well-earned trip was now before Shylo and Jim. They had slept in, taking advantage of the motel's late checkout time, and were now on their way. The thrill of getting on a motorcycle and going on a trip has been talked about, but the excitement of a thirteen-year-old boy traveling in a truck is something you just have to be a thirteen-year-old boy to experience. This feeling doesn't exist so much from arriving, but more from just going. To witness and experience all the different sights, cultures, climates, human achievements and various product that each state has to offer is a marvel to behold.

By noon they had gone through the Georgia and Tennessee port of entry and stopped on the outskirts of Chattanooga to have breakfast. After a leisurely meal and fueling up, they were on their way again. Shylo asked, "What does a port of entry do?"

"Three things. They make sure you have the rights and are licensed to cross their state. If not, then they sell you a temporary permit. If you are a motor carrier, making money by hauling whatever, then they deserve monies for services supplied, such as roads and law enforcement. Second, they check to make sure you're not overweight, since this is hard on the asphalt. Third, they check your logbook and make sure that you are responsible to maintain, to see if you are within the eligible hours to drive, so you don't fall asleep at the wheel."

Jim surveyed the straight, vacant, sloping road and asked Shylo, "Okay, hotshot, do you think you're tall enough to reach the pedals and see over the steering wheel at the same time?"

Shylo had been waiting for this moment since they left home. He just grinned and eagerly shook his head yes.

Jim said, "We'll see." He eased the unit off the side of the road and came to a stop. "First of all, don't let the size of the vehicle intimidate you; the clutch, brake and gas work just like a car. It takes more force to start and stop the truck because of the weight. A heavy car is five thousand pounds; right now we weigh over fifty thousand pounds. The two air valves on the dash are parking brakes, the red is for the tractor, and the blue is for the trailer. The silver lever on the steering column applies the brakes to the trailer only, where the foot pedal applies the brakes to the tractor and trailer. Maybe we shouldn't get into so much all at once, since it can be confusing."

They traded seats. Shylo's heart was pumping wildly, giving him a sick feeling in the bottom of his stomach. He kept telling himself that he shouldn't do it. *He expects too much of me; something is going to happen.*

Jim asked, "Are you okay?"

"Of course, Dad, I couldn't be better."

Jim paused, took a heavy breath and spoke. "Remember, if anything happens, keep both hands on the wheel and come to a stop. Now, slide your seat closer to the steering wheel and sit on this."

He handed Shylo a small pillow and explained, "The first two gears break inertia and gets your unit moving. The rest of the gears build up speed. Try to keep the tachometer in the green. If the needle reaches the yellow, your RPM is too high. You're over rapping the motor and need to go to the next highest gear. If the needle is in the red, the RPM is too low and you're lugging the motor and need to go to the next lowest gear."

Shylo replied, "Red down, yellow up, I got you. What could go wrong?"

He put the gearshift in second gear with the button down like he had been observing.

Jim acknowledged, "That's right, start out in second. First is deep under for hills."

Shylo looked both ways, not just to see if anything was coming or going, but to make sure nothing was in sight. He came up off the clutch slowly and pressed on the fuel, almost too hard. Still maintaining control, he eased onto the pavement and pulled up on the red button. Letting up on the gas and pressing down again, the truck changed gears smoothly. Jim grinned and nodded his head in approval without looking at Shylo. Quickly, the tachometer needle approached the yellow. Shylo let off the gas, pulled the gearshift to neutral, double clutched, pulled the shift into third then let off the clutch. He pressed the button and pushed the gas down in the same motion; the truck did not go into gear. Instead it made a clicking noise like a piece of cardboard, hitting the spokes of a bicycle.

Shylo said, "Oops, what happened?"

Jim spoke slowly, making sure Shylo did not act out of confusion. "Push the clutch in and come to a stop."

Jim grinned. "That's a hard one to learn. It's kind of like rubbing your head and patting your stomach at the same time. Remember that button operates a gear in the rear end, and it takes a brief moment for it to kick in or disengage. Let's try that again."

Shylo went back through the same process again. This time he tried to forget about the button until the gearshift was in place. There was a moment of clicking before it slammed into gear.

Jim acknowledged the sound by saying, "Too slow."

Thirty minutes later he was using the button with no clicking noise. Shylo asked, "Why is there a trailer brake on the steering column?"

"It comes in handy at lights or taking off on a hill. On a hill, pull the lever down to apply the trailer brakes. When you're ready to go, slowly let up on the clutch until it starts to take hold, then push on the fuel and let up on the lever accordingly. If you jackknife, that lever can be a lifesaver. When you jackknife, the trailer starts to slide sideways around the tractor. If you use the foot brake at all it will just get worse. So you need to slowly apply the trailer brake and push down on the gas pedal to pull yourself straight."

Jim looked at the highway that was now starting to come alive with other vehicles. "Maybe you better let me have it back before we reach Nashville."

Shylo eased off the side of the road with the gearshift in neutral. He applied both parking brakes and looked at Jim for a report. Jim said, "Good job, my man, good job."

Jim resumed his position behind the wheel. Shylo's heartbeat returned to normal as the feeling of his successful driving overwhelmed his entire body.

You know the feeling, the one that comes with the knowledge that you can do something. The rest of the day would shine if the sun were out or not.

Jim smiled at the sight of his son. Not that he could read his mind, but that he knew the state of Shylo's gratification by the straight-lipped grin on his face. The two rolled down the highway, each with their arm in the window, as usual. Before long, Jim's left arm and Shylo's right arm would be sunburned. The evidence of a crowded city gave appearance as the tight little roads became more and more inhabited by vehicles.

Shylo remembered the last time he saw Nashville, and the contrast there now was. Last summer they had driven through the city at two o'clock in the morning. They were the only vehicle in sight, let alone the only one moving. The streets looked very small, but they were so clean you would have thought somebody washed them before going to bed. He recollected driving up to the front of the Grand Ole Opry, and the night watchman allowing them to step inside to see the center stage. He remembered the large red velvet-looking curtain across the stage. It was the largest curtain he had ever seen.

Memories and thoughts were broken as Jim asked a question. "Hey, bud, you think there's somewhere around here we can get some grits and hog back? The biscuits and gravy are just about gone."

"I would imagine these old country boys got something in the fridge."

"Yeah, well, the question is where's the fridge?"

Completely out of context, Jim continues. "You know, it's funny, out of all the states, rock 'n' roll and country live in the same one. If we ever go to Memphis we'll go see Graceland, even if we only get to stand in front and look."

Jim pointed down the street and announced, "Well, how about that, food for men." Shylo looked and saw the hamburger stand, appropriately named Big John's Hamburgers.

Jim pulled off in a lot beside the stand and gave Shylo some money. "This is good; I can bring my log book up to snuff while you get us something to eat. I'll take two cheeseburgers, fries and a Coke." Shylo left quickly.

A few minutes later he returned, as Jim sat waiting. "I hope we remembered ketchup?"

"We did."

The two talked to each other about life in general as they ate and enjoyed each other's company.

A short time later, with nothing left but the ice in their drinks, Shylo stuffed everything into the paper sack to throw away later.

Jim said, "Let's see if we can make another mile." This was always what he said, instead of "Let's go." He turned the key and nothing happened; he let go, then tried again, but there was still nothing.

"Uh-oh, boss, I think we got a problem." He tried the headlights and turn signal. They worked okay. He got out, raised the split hood on the passengers side and looked at the battery and wires, then crawled underneath and looked at the starter and wiring. All looked okay; he called to Shylo for a hammer. He retrieved the tool out of the jock box on the side of the tractor and handed it underneath to Jim, who hit the side of the starter with two medium strikes. He crawled out from underneath, got in and tried the key again.

Bang! The motor kicked over and came to life. He grinned and replied, "I like that old saying, 'If it's electrical and won't work, hit it and try again.' We'll see if we can get that fixed tomorrow, before we end up stranded in the middle of nowhere." He got out to lower the hood, first looking underneath to make sure all was in place. Then he got back in and asked, "Are we ready?"

"Yes."

"It'll be a lot easier to get that done tomorrow instead of tonight. It's going on six p.m. Well, in those famous, immortal two words, 'To Oz,'" he said, as he pointed ahead of him.

They were underway again.

Jim pulled back on the pavement and talked as if to get Shylo's approval for his reasoning. "We only have an hour left to Clarksville. Maybe there we can find the International shop and spend the night close, so we can have that starter fixed the first thing tomorrow. But then again, Nashville is a big place; maybe we would be smarter to find a place here and park close."

Shylo said, "Here."

"Okay, let's find a phone booth, get the address and see if we can find the place."

Two hours later, after going around the same block twice, they were in front of the International shop. The sign said open, and Jim went inside. A few moments later he returned. Getting back in the truck and grinning, he replied, "Next time, remind me to invest a dime and call first. Anyway, they have a night crew, and the mechanic said to let it sit still for about twenty minutes and he'd be out to look at it. Another starter costs fifty dollars and only takes a matter of minutes to change out."

Two hours later they left with a new starter. "What we need now is a place to park for the night."

A few minutes later Jim pulled into an empty lot, came to a stop and laughed as he pointed ahead. Shylo followed the direction of his finger and laughed too when he saw the sign—Big John's Hamburgers.

Jim acknowledged, "This must be what they mean when they say, 'Spinning your wheels and going nowhere.' Oh well, it could have been worse. If they hadn't had that starter in stock, we could have been stuck there all day tomorrow."

Hotel rooms were only for work that would last more than one day or layovers. They walked to the back of the trailer and opened one of the doors. A partial tier with a stack of pads was at the back doors.

Jim said, "Give me three of those pads to go across the seats, and I'll take the cab while you have the trailer."

The next morning came and all Shylo remembered was lying down. Jim was pulling at Shylo's pant leg, saying, "Hey, Popeye, we still need to find a place to eat."

Shylo rebounded, and a moment later had his shoes on and was standing in front of Jim.

"We'll make sure it's a truck stop, top off the tanks, call dispatch and do it."

Jim worked for Baker Moving, but on the road was dispatched by Red Horse Van Lines. Baker's prime carrier was out of Louisville, Kentucky, and had paid a percentage to paint all of Baker's equipment red and white, with black lettering of both company names behind an enormous red stallion. His head was way too small in proportion to his body. From the front left corner he stood with a noble stance, with his head up and his mane flowing in the breeze. The passenger's side was the same scene, only with the horse's right front so that he could always be facing the front of any unit. Not counting the front or back of a trailer, it took more red paint than white to paint it. The tractor was all red. Baker had three trucks on the road for Red Horse.

Jim was responsible to call Red Horse dispatch every morning and after every delivery, but he was only required to call the Baker office when he felt it was necessary for money or anytime there were new instructions, or the old instructions changed. Baker had a good reason for this. Red Horse, like any prime carrier, had two types of drivers. There were owner operators, who owned or were buying the tractor and pulling Red Horse's trailer, and agent drivers, like Jim, who drove an agent's equipment. Some loads look good, but go into an area that's hard to get a load out of, such as large retirement areas, and Red Horse paid dead head mileage, which is empty mileage to secure a load. But this wasn't enough to be considered break-even money. So, unlike the owner operator, Jim, who represented Baker, couldn't turn the load down or at least barter for future loads. Mr. Baker, who knew less about it than Jim, or his other two drivers, could and would refuse a load, or, as the proper term would be, turn a load back to dispatch.

This morning, Jim wanted to let Mr. Baker know about the fifty dollar starter, so that in the near future, when he needed money wired out, the boss would have some idea where his money was going.

With all things taken care of, Jim announced as he put the truck in gear, "The program is to cross the Mississippi river by one p.m. and be pushing Kansas City by nightfall. Are we ready? Then let's make another mile."

When the vehicle was on clear road and was at a normal pace between fifth high and fifth low, Shylo asked, "Why do you bump the tires when you stop?"

"You should do it every time you get out of the vehicle. In fact, every couple of hours this should be done to check for a flat tire. You can tear up a flat tire next to a good tire and never know it until you see the rubber flying away in your mirror. When you bump the tire it makes a certain thump. If all the wheels are up to par, you'll get the same sound and feel with a piece of pipe or a solid stick. If a tire is real low or flat, you'll be able to tell it. The problem is, a tire can go flat or start to peel at any time, and after ten to fifteen miles of steady, hard running it can disintegrate. That's why it's important to bump your tires."

Shylo leaned back and went, "Oh, I thought you could tell when a tire went flat."

Jim grinned. "Well, you can if it's a front one."

Shylo grinned and said, "Yeah."

A few moments later Jim admitted, "Single axles are a lot easier to detect a problem then tandems."

"What's a tandem?"

"Two axles instead of one."

The area was heavily wooded, but the road was straight and vacant. Jim gave Shylo a second look and said, "Okay, thumper, are we ready for this?"

Shylo's face went flush with excitement as he answered, "Yes, we are."

With a visibility of more than a mile in front and in the mirrors, Jim stopped, set his flashers and stopped in the middle of his lane on the two-lane road. He switched places with Shylo.

Shylo's arms and legs felt weak as he put the truck into gear, released the two parking brakes and turned the flashers off. He knew he would be okay if he could just get the vehicle moving. The clutch pedal came up, the fuel pedal went down and the truck started lurching like a grasshopper.

Jim reached over and pulled the trailer brake down part way. The motor died, and the truck stopped. Jim grinned. "That's another thing that brake is good for—student drivers."

Jim stopped grinning when he saw the hurt look on Shylo's face. "Okay, okay, it's not that big a deal. Take a second, collect your thoughts, concentrate and try again." Shylo started the motor and pushed in on the two brake valves that had not been pulled out.

Jim said, "First, press down a little on the gas a couple times so you can coordinate that resistance with the clutch." Shylo complied, Jim reached over and released the brake on the steering column.

"Now, let's try that again." The truck moved forward, and Shylo went through the gears without a flaw. Jim acknowledged this with enthusiasm.

"All right, that works so good we're going to put it in the unwritten book of instructions."

1964
THE WORLD TURNS

CHaPTer one

Shylo looked out the window as the Greyhound bus rolled down the highway. His memory went back to the previous summer, to the adventures of traveling and working for his father. Although he didn't get any further west than Denver, Colorado, he had still seen a lot of states between the Mile High City and the East Coast, including Texas and Florida. Jim never knew where he was headed next, until he made a delivery and talked to dispatch. Then, any new shipment had to fall in line with the space he had available in the trailer, and the destinations and delivery dates of whatever shipments he still had on board. Shylo had experienced a good summer last year. Jim paid him a dollar and twenty-five cents an hour, and for all necessities. Shylo paid for his extras such as movies and the like. He still managed to take home two hundred dollars for new school clothes, and even bought Cannon two new outfits and a pair of shoes.

This year, school had already been out for five days, and Jim had been gone for over two weeks and was now in Memphis, Tennessee, loading for Ft. Worth, Texas. Because of the lack of interstate shipments with Red Horse Van Lines, Jim had endured a very slow winter. During the slow season, for three months he had been forced to work part time locally, taking work away from the full time local employees at Baker Moving and Storage. But with all this over and done, the world turns, taking no knowledge or making no memory to the ill-fated past.

Jim proposed to buy Shylo a bus ticket to meet him in Memphis—he could bring his advance money from the Baker office instead of it being sent by

Western Union. The bus made a turn into the Memphis terminal, and Shylo watched for Jim. When the vehicle came to a full stop, there was Jim, waiting where the passengers would get out.

Shylo retrieved his suitcase and bag and went to greet his dad. A moment of awkwardness went by as Shylo stood in front of Jim, holding his luggage. He dropped his bags and hugged his father anyway. Before picking them back up he handed Jim the money he had been carrying in his front pocket. Jim secured it in his wallet, helped Shylo with his luggage, and they left without a word being said.

CHAPTER TWO

Jim had loaded fifteen thousand pounds, three-fourths the trailer, for Ft. Worth, Texas, and had the promise of two large shipments out of Ft. Worth to Denver, Colorado. Throwing the luggage in the trailer and then climbing into the International Loadstar, they wanted to get out of town before rush hour, stop and eat, and then get a good head start on the next day's drive of five hundred miles.

After crossing the great Mississippi river, stopping at both ports in Tennessee and Arkansas, and stopping to eat, they continued on. While they traveled, Shylo asked Jim, "What's the problem with Mr. Baker? When he gave me your expense money, he said he just couldn't afford to keep dishing out money to you."

Jim replied, "I'll tell you what his problem is. He puts me out here in this piece of junk that keeps breaking down. It doesn't even have a sleeper and should only be a local truck to begin with. Every time it breaks down, he's the one who pays for it, but he tries to make me feel guilty, like it's my fault and I'm taking the food right off his table. Well, it's not my fault; and just between you and me, I'll tell you what I just made up my mind to do about it. Last week, when I was broken down with a bad air compressor in Odessa, Texas, I was offered a job, and I have decided to take it. Mr. Matthew, the owner of Best Way Moving, the Red Horse agent in Odessa, wants me to be his new operations manager. At the end of August his old manager is going to retire, and Mr. Matthew wants me to take over his position. His company is about the same size as Baker's, but there I would be the manager, the local dispatcher and responsible for operations. If the job was at home I would have jumped at it, but moving to Texas made it a bit more complicated. I told him I'd have to think it over and talk with my wife first. He said that was good, and to just let him know when I made a decision. Well, the thinking over part is done, and all that's left is talking to your mom. Tell me what you think about moving to Texas."

Shylo cleared his throat and looked at Jim with a smile. "Sounds good to me."

Jim grinned and nodded his head before he said, "I was hoping you would say that."

Darkness had overtaken the land, and Little Rock, Arkansas, was within twenty miles when Jim pulled over into a large vacant area to park for the night. After taking care of necessary business and brushing their teeth, they prepared to bed down in the back of the trailer. Jim locked the padlock on the handle of the door that was open, then blocked the door open a few inches for air with a folded burlap and tied it shut from inside. Taking their shoes and socks off, they climbed onto a stack of furniture pads each, for a well-deserved night of sleep.

Shylo had missed the comfort of sleeping on those pads. While Jim turned the flashlight off, Shylo spoke, "Don't let me forget to fill up the water cooler tomorrow; the thing's near about empty."

Naturally, Jim grunted an okay, but then he looked in the dark to Shylo's direction and thought, *I think I just got disciplined.*

The following day was an easy task of three hundred miles, with Shylo driving part of the way across the flat land. He remembered all he had been taught the previous year, and was now big enough that he didn't need a small pillow to see over the wheel.

It was early afternoon as they approached the last fifty miles to Dallas and then thirty miles to Ft. Worth. As they traveled, Shylo surveyed the land through the passenger's window, looking at the bluebonnet flowers that grew wild on the side of the highway. The existence of trees was erratic. One moment, trees were mildly abundant; the next time you paid attention there wasn't a tree in sight. This was part of the character of Texas that helped to make up its personality. The most impressive thing about every state was they all had a different culture and personality.

"Hey, pancake."

Shylo looked to see what Jim wanted. Jim pointed ahead, and Shylo watched the vehicle coming in the other lane. Something was wrong. It looked like the front of a trailer, with a windshield, a radiator fixture, headlights and a bumper, but the thing had no fenders or hood. With a deep-seated, continuous roar, it flashed by, growling for its share of the road. Following it, Shylo's head turned and he replied, "Wow! What was that?"

"That was a cab-over diesel."

Shylo, his forehead wrinkled, with his head tilted down and his eyes looking up, looked at Jim.

Jim continued. "That type of truck is becoming more popular all the time, and you can definitely see its advantages. Basically, there are now two types of trucks to pull a trailer with—the cab-over and the conventional. The cab-over has the motor under the cab with a hump, or doghouse, between the two seats to provide room for it. The conventional has the motor in front, with fenders and hood. Without the fenders and hood, the cab-over is obviously shorter. If your maximum overall length with a trailer is forty-five feet, and you have a ten-foot cab-over in front, then you can pull a thirty-five-foot trailer. If you have a fifteen-foot conventional in front, you can only pull a thirty-foot trailer. Your equipment should be geared to your load. But, the big controversy here is that if you hit something head-on with a cab-over, the point of impact is at the windshield, and you don't have anything out front to cushion or absorb the blow. Now, the other side of that argument is that, with a conventional, the fenders and hood might crush like a cushion, but that big, hot motor will get pushed right back up in your lap." He looked at Shylo, who was listening intently.

"Okay, enough for body styles. Let's talk about the big, bad diesel. This motor is going to be the wave of the future for trucks. Like the gas motor, it's a four-cycle, internal combustion engine, but it runs on diesel fuel, not gas. Diesel is oil, and oil is more highly combustible than gas. Gas uses a spark plug and diesel doesn't. On the compression stroke, the fuel is ignited by pressure. This happens at about five degrees before top dead center, forcing the piston back down. The understanding is that you can't lay a nickel flat between the piston and the head when the piston is at TDC."

CHaPTer THree

Four days later, Shylo and Jim were headed for Denver, Colorado. Their fifteen thousand pounds had delivered into storage, and the two shipments for Denver were loaded in one day each at residences in Ft. Worth. The only difference was the estimated seven thousand pound load actually went four thousand and forty pounds, and the estimated eight thousand went eleven thousand nine hundred and eighty pounds. Loading the smaller shipment first was a short day, and Jim showed Shylo how to inventory and tag each item of a shipment.

Leaving the Fort Worth area, Jim remarked, "We have a little under eight hundred miles to Denver; two easy days of sightseeing. It's funny how we ended up with fifteen thousand pounds. I'm sure glad that eight went almost twelve, or we would have ended up only half full, and if the eight had gone like the seven, it would have been bad!"

Irrationally, he changed the subject. "It's too bad Odessa is so far out of the way; we could go visit Mr. Matthew at Best Way Moving. He was born and raised in the Lone Star State and told me some of its history. Other states relied on the railroad for growth, but for the territory of Texas the railroad was a must. The equation of settlements and railroad was a hard one to overcome. Without the railroad there could be no settlements, and without the settlements there was no reason for a railroad. Before Odessa was conceived, the Western Union Telegraph and Union Pacific laid track through it. A crew of three hundred and fifty laborers, mostly Irish and Chinese workers, using twenty-four cars of track, seventy-five cars of ties and twelve cars of water daily, pitched camp at mile marker two hundred and ninety-six. Having a drink at this place to bring the day's hard work to an end marked the milepost, which eventually became the new town of Odessa. In the late eighteen hundreds the railroad took care of the ranchers, and in the early nineteen hundreds it took care of the oilfield. Odessa, a central point in Texas, became a large distribution center for oilfield equipment."

Jim looked at Shylo and pulled off the road. "We may as well take advantage of this flat, open country.

"I have been waiting patiently."

"To drive or take care of business?"

"Both."

They both took a quick jaunt in the bush for personal privacy, and they climbed back in. Shylo said, "Okay, let's make a mile." Jim smiled and nodded his head.

A few moments later, Shylo had it back on the road, going between fifth high and fifth low to keep the tachometer in the green.

Acknowledging the success of his son's driving ability, Jim said, "The next thing you're going to have to learn is how to back up. You can tell how much driving experience a person has just by the way they pull up to back in. First of all, always back in on the driver's side, even if you have to go around the block If you have to back in on the blind side, make sure you have a responsible person guiding you. And remember, if they can't see you in the mirror, you can't see them, and any time you can't see them, don't move. If you're backing into a driveway or whatever, come down the road with the driveway on your left. Turn like you're going into it, but when you get close, turn and go back out into your lane. When you get back into the right lane, turn again to the left and stop at the curb, making a backward "S." You do all this with a mechanical slowness, taking into consideration the length of your unit, so when you come to a stop the back of the trailer is lined up with the front of the driveway and you're already turned in the position to push the trailer in. All you have to do is turn the wheel to the right or left to adjust your direction. Turn to the right and the back of the trailer goes to the left, turn to the left and it goes to the right. If you watch someone with a lot of experience, they even pull their car up like this to back in. When we get the opportunity, we'll have to practice this."

Late the next day, a Saturday, they arrived in the outlying area of Denver and acquired a room where Jim had stayed before, the Honolulu Inn. Jim's immediate problem was laundry, and he knew where to have it done. So they bagged their dirty clothes and walked to Won Cleaners. The apprehensive-looking Chinese lady behind the counter explained that she wouldn't be able to have the clothes back until Monday. She told them there was a new process called dry cleaning that would cost a little more, but she could have their apparel back tomorrow. Shylo asked if the dry cleaning would work on Levis. She moved her head to the left, right, up and down and replied, "Of course."

The following day, Shylo did something he had never done before. While Jim was busy reading a book, he went to a movie by himself. He went to see the opening day of *West Side Story*. If he had known it was a musical, if he had read more than just the name of the movie in the paper, he would not have gone. But after watching the film long enough to become interested, the music intrigued him and the storyline captured his devoted attention. By the end of the sequence of events between the Jets and the Sharks, he found himself avoiding eye contact with people during his walk back to the room. He would have been embarrassed for anyone to see his emotions.

CHAPTER FOUR

On Monday morning both shipments were cleared for storage at Archibald Movers in Denver, and were unloaded that day. Tuesday turned into a day of waiting for a load to develop.

On Wednesday morning an estimated ten thousand registered in Salt Lake City, Utah, for the L.A. area. With eight thousand pounds in the Archibald warehouse going to San Francisco, this made a load.

By six o'clock Wednesday evening, Archibald's shipment had been loaded, hamburgers had been eaten, and they were making their way west on the highway. They stopped that night, and the next morning continued up and down over the Rocky Mountains.

Jim said, "Five hundred and sixty-five miles of mountains between Denver and Salt Lake. It is a beautiful drive in the summer, but I can tell you for a fact that you don't come this way in the winter. The snow will bury you alive. From the first of October to the middle of April you go up north and use another highway through Wyoming. Not that it's a whole lot better; you're just less likely to get snowed in until spring."

He looked over at Shylo. Jim was grinning, but Shylo looked dead serious. He continued, saying, "They say in Wyoming it only snows once, and then spends the rest of the year blowing around. And you don't worry what the temperature is—you worry what the wind chill factor is. Right now they're busy constructing a new freeway up there, Interstate Eighty, a divided highway with two lanes on each side, reaching a fabulous distance of almost three thousand miles. It will go nonstop between the East and West Coast when it's completed."

"Wow, you mean when it's done, if you could carry enough gas, you could drive non-stop between the Atlantic and Pacific Ocean?" Shylo asked.

"Barring road construction, that was the understanding I got."

As fast as he could, Shylo did the math in his head. Three thousand miles at five miles a gallon. He looked up at Jim before he spoke. "Instead of those two thirty-five gallon saddle tanks it would take two three hundred gallon tanks."

"With diesel fuel being so much cheaper than gas, that's another big plus for the diesel."

The end of June provided a comfortable temperature to travel through the mountains, but the narrow road commanded attention as it darted from side to side and constantly went either up or down. Late in the evening, when they reached the highway going over Parley's canyon and down into the city of Salt Lake, Jim asked, "How's that brake working over there?"

Shylo ignored him and asked, "What's the plan, Dad?"

"Well, another twenty miles down the hill and we're going to find a place to enjoy a long, easy dinner. We'll park in front of Sims Moving tonight, so bright and early in the morning we'll be there first thing."

The next day the estimated ten thousand pounds went a little over twelve thousand pounds. Late that evening they returned from loading to park in front of Sims Moving so they could have their paperwork done the first thing Saturday morning.

CHAPTER FIVE

The sun was coming up behind the trailer as they went across the Salt Flats. Shylo said, "It's remarkable how you come out of such tall mountains onto such a flat land."

Jim pointed to the side of the road, at the Great Salt Lake. "I think it's the largest body of inland saltwater in America. It's one of the first things for every tourist to see in Utah. They look at it and say, 'Wow, that's something else,' but they leave their camera in its case. And as soon as they get a good smell of the lake, they decide to leave. Let's have one of those guaranteed fresh donuts we bought this morning, and in a couple of hours we'll stop in Nevada for one of those famous cheap meals."

While they traveled, Shylo looked at the words written with rocks on the flat, white, salt-covered land next to the road. "Dad, where did all those stones come from?"

"I have a sneaky suspicion they got hauled in from somewhere else. When you look at what's laying on the side of the road there just doesn't seem to be that many, but maybe that's where they went to in the first place."

"They should have used some of them to fill up the gigantic holes in this road."

"We could suggest that, but I don't think anyone would listen. Do you?"

At one p.m. they walked out of one of the two casinos in Wendover, Nevada. Jim looked up at the sun and shook his head. "Man, it's hard to leave the inside of that cool building!"

Shylo followed him, holding his stomach with both hands. "I don't think I've ever seen that much good food, and I wish I hadn't been such a little pig before coming out into this heat!"

Jim spoke with a large frown. "To make it even worse, we're headed for the hottest part of Nevada in the hottest part of the day. Oh well, when we get out of Nevada we'll be back in the mountains. Until then we'll just have to use the air conditioner."

"What air conditioner?"

"Two windows and forty miles an hour."

They both grinned. Before leaving, they stopped at the truck stop to fuel up, and for the first time Jim let Shylo drive away from a populated area. This responsibility was a big deal to Shylo and put an imaginary seal of approval on his ability.

That night they parked in the Sierra Mountains, just before starting the climb up over Donner's Pass.

The next morning started with a hard pull up the nearly seven percent grade. Everyone passed in the middle lane while Jim used the right lane for slow-moving vehicles. Finally, they topped the hill and started to pick up speed. Shylo looked ahead, looked back at Jim, and then looked ahead again. He couldn't believe what he saw: a large protruding rock from the adjacent hill on the right was hanging over the lane they had to be in. You could see that a car would fit under it, but a twelve-feet high trailer was definitely in grave doubt. And to make it worse, it was in the middle of a hard right curve. There was no way you could see what was coming.

He looked at Jim again, who didn't seem concerned. You could see the oncoming lane around the curve from the driver's seat, but he refused to let Shylo know this. With a childish mischief, Jim ignored his concern. Shylo watched intently, and just before reaching the overhang, Jim eased about halfway over the double yellow line. The oncoming lane remained empty, but if someone had been coming they would have been forced off the pavement.

Shylo swallowed hard and asked, "Is that lane always empty?"

"Everyone always seems to fit."

A few hours later and they were going south on 101. The International Harvest Show was taking place in the center of San Francisco. This was an outside event in the streets that took place every summer to show off new implements. There was mostly farm equipment, but also new vehicles of all kinds, and inventions that would be marketed to consumers. Jim was anxious to reach the agent, drop the trailer and bobtail to where they could get out and walk to observe whatever was on display.

After crossing the historical Golden Gate Bridge, they dropped the trailer next to Bay Side Movers. Then they found the center of action, parked and walked to the displays. The dominating factor of the event was definitely the shiny green farm machinery.

CHapTer six

The trick was to figure out what each machine did, and this was accomplished by reading the plaque in front of the display. There were plaques up the gazoo. It didn't take long to stop reading all the endless information and just look at the interesting shapes and sizes of the new dark green machinery.

Eventually the path led to a scaffold built around the front of a cab-over, gas turbine Ford truck. The scaffold allowed you to see through the windows but not go inside. The sight through the windows was years beyond its time. The jet airplane-style steering wheel made you look twice. Jim questioned, "That wouldn't work at all for a hand-over-hand turn."

Behind the wheel was a large U-shaped console going around the front and right side of the driver. The passenger's seat was an ultra-modern reclining chair with access to a television on the left. Behind the seats was the concept of a walk-in closet without doors. To the right was a large place for hanging clothes amid the various built-in shelves and drawers. To the left was a counter with three large silver pots, like the ones behind the counter in a café. To the right of these was a sink and a built-in mini-refrigerator. Above this were cupboards with drawers underneath. Behind this area was a door to exit the vehicle from the sleeper on the passenger's side, and a small permanent desk with a seat on the driver's side. Still further behind this was a large built-in bed.

Jim remarked, "Nobody would ever be able to afford it. You could buy three trucks for what that one would cost." They exited the scaffold and continued walking and looking, but nothing else seemed to capture their attention like the Ford truck.

Late that evening they returned to their own truck and started it. As usual, they sat there for a moment, waiting for the air gauge to build up over sixty pounds and release the brakes. Shylo looked up and remarked, "A walk-in closet!"

"Yeah, the thing was pretty impressive to a couple of country bumpkins like us." They then drove to Fisherman's Wharf to enjoy one of its famous fish dinners.

The next morning Shylo found out what first gear was for. The eight thousand pounds delivered out to the suburb area of the city, and more than once Jim was forced to stop on one of the city's monstrously steep hills. Each time, Shylo knew they were in trouble, but each time Jim used first gear and finished the climb at a speed that you really could get out and walk faster than.

Shylo informed Jim, "I see now why they call first gear 'deep under.' It must have been invented for this city."

Jim replied, "No, actually, it can also be very helpful when you get stuck in the mud or snow."

The residence had a two-flight carry up twenty steps before reaching the house, and the house was two levels. Jim hired an extra man from the agent for help. He didn't work for the agent, but was a lot worker, or a lumper, who worked for drivers. After a short time of carrying furniture up the stairs, Jim remarked, "Being a mover in this city will either make a man out of you or kill you."

CHaPTer seven

The following morning found Shylo and Jim going south to L.A. on Interstate 5. "I'm glad both our shipments didn't deliver in Frisco."

Shylo spoke while he flexed his sore arms. "Well, I'm just glad the small one delivered there. With any luck the big one will go into storage at the agent in Los Angeles." Jim grinned and nodded his head in a reassuring gesture.

Of course, at the agent, the twelve thousand pound shipment cleared for direct delivery to the Lakewood area of L.A., and Jim hired one extra man. There were no stairs or long carries to the one-level home, but twelve thousand pounds was the equivalent of a twelve-room house, and a lot of work to unload, set up, reassemble and unpack

Thursday morning made for a much more exciting day. Jim was assigned both an eight and nine thousand pound shipment, in storage at a foreign carrier, Mel Mack Moving in Santa Anna. Both shipments were bound for Ft. Bragg in Fayetteville, North Carolina.

En route to load, Shylo saw a sign he would see many more times through out his life. It read: "Disneyland Next 3 Exits."

They loaded the smaller of the two shipments that day, and Friday morning, before loading the second, Jim called dispatch as usual. A small twenty-five hundred pounds for Ft. Bragg, North Carolina, awaited Jim at the Archibald warehouse in Denver. He was happy as he and Shylo finished loading the second shipment.

"It's about time things started falling in place. Saturday and Sunday to make Denver, load the twenty-five hundred Monday morning that will fill us out, and we'll be home by Thursday night. We'll have a three-day weekend at home on Friday, Saturday and Sunday."

CHAPTER EIGHT

At eight o'clock that evening the large red horse on the right side of the trailer seemed to be watching with full attention. Between the trees and curves a massive spectacle was coming into view on the right side of the road. The Hoover Dam, a gigantic wall of cement between two mountains that created Lake Mead, loomed ahead. When the dam was in full sight, Jim shook Shylo, who had fallen asleep in an awkward, upright position. Still asleep, he spoke out loud.

"STOP! STOP! Slow down! Slow down!"

He shook him again. His eyes came open, but for a few seconds nothing registered in the brain. Finally, he rubbed both eyes and said, "What?"

Jim pointed to the right, and Shylo looked. His head lifted, and his eyes opened wide.

"Wow, what's that? A brace between the mountains?"

"No, that's Hoover Dam."

"Wow, how did they make that?"

"I don't know, but I wish I had what all that cement cost."

A half-hour later they made their way into Las Vegas, Nevada.

chapter nine

Jim had decided on a room for the night so they could see some of the sights and leave in the morning. The highway went straight through the center of town, with a stop light at every corner.

"I forget which one, but one of these casinos has a display of antique cars. But first we must be fed, and anyone who knows where to eat in Vegas goes to the basement of the Silver Slipper for their buffet. There's a chef in white linen at the end of their buffet line to cut off your selection of the best tasting prime rib you ever ate. And the price comes out of your front pocket, not your back."

The absence of the sun made it comfortable to put your arm in the window, and the combination of lights and glitter captured Shylo's attention. The smell of the day's hot pavement still hung heavy in the air, and a sound came at them of someone in front of a casino with a cane, top hat and circus attire yelling at anyone walking by on the sidewalk, "Come in and get rich!"

Jim said, "At one time the biggest casinos were having such a war for gamblers they actually gave away breakfast, until the restaurants that had no gambling got together and forced the gaming commission to stop this practice. But what really made the free breakfast so great was that you didn't even have to gamble!" Jim shook his head and laughed.

They pulled into the large dirt lot of the casino with a gigantic high heel on top of the building. They had arrived at the "Silver Slipper."

Jim said again as they climbed out, "This place is just like the rest of them. Anyone under twenty-one has to stay within the specially marked lines in the

45

carpet when walking through the gambling area. Follow me, I've been here before."

Shylo's hunger was forgotten as he entered the buffet room. The casino upstairs was elaborate, but this was just plain elegant, like the beautiful girl wearing expensive jewelry at the Academy Awards. In spite of the fact that no girl was there in an evening gown or glass high heeled shoes, he could see where they got the name "Silver Slipper." Everything except the tables was upholstered in red velvet. The tablecloths were a starched white that reached almost to the floor, and the backs of the antique-looking chairs extended above your head when you sat down. The intermittently placed crystal chandeliers hung at different heights from the ceiling, and the walls seemed to be made of one large, continuous mirror. The long buffet table held more entrees than you could ever remember, let alone eat. Smaller tables contained the salads and desserts. Even though he felt like a poor man in a rich man's place, he meditated, "Now this is the place I would like to bring a girl either before or after the school dance."

Jim touched Shylo's shoulder. "Get a little white cup of their special horseradish to go on the prime rib. It's hot and strong but delicious."

"What do you eat with prime rib?"

"Well, I'm going to have a baked potato with sour cream, some asparagus, a roll, some clam chowder soup and a salad. That should fill up any ugly person."

"Sounds good to me."

At the end of the table was a person cutting the prime rib. He wore a white linen robe that matched the tablecloths, and a large white bakery hat.

Jim leaned over and whispered, "The rare meat is the best."

Shylo looked at the man in white with a large fork and knife, who awaited his word. "Your rarest cut, please." The man grinned so large that he had to open his mouth as he cut off a slice of meat. Shylo grinned and shook his head yes when he observed that it didn't matter what you asked for; you were still going to get the same slice of meat. The chef couldn't speak a word of English.

The aroma and sight of the good food was a pleasure to enjoy as they found a table and sat down. Shylo was anxious to try the mixture of horseradish and meat. His eyes and nostrils popped open as it slid down his throat. He grabbed the glass of ice water and tried to chase the burning hot substance. His eyes flooded up like the water had gone the wrong way, and he covered his mouth while he sat there choking.

"Man, that stuff is as bad as Chinese mustard!"

"I told you it was strong."

His next bite of meat was without the horseradish. It tasted every bit as good as it looked and smelled. While he proceeded to eat the soup and salad, the desire for the right amount of the radish grew, but he left it alone. By the time he finished, the only way he could take another bite was if the item was chocolate, like chocolate pie, ice cream or even the exquisite chocolate-covered strawberries.

CHAPTER TEN

Like Jim planned, Monday morning they loaded the twenty-five hundred pounds out of Archibald's warehouse in Denver, Colorado. Shylo suspected that his dad possessed a sixth sense when it came to his schedules. The small shipment filled the van so full that the walk board, piano board, two wheeler and four wheeler had to be tied on the back of the trailer. The side door to the back on the passenger's side contained an open-faced wooden box big enough for luggage. It was on the floor, in the load, against the wheelhouse facing the door. The only time the box was moved was when access through the door was required. Otherwise, it held their luggage when the van was full.

With the final chore accomplished and the sun overhead, father and son were sitting in the let's go position. Jim expressed an enthusiastic expression and said, "Let's make a mile."

The groan of a heavy-laden vehicle pulled out on the pavement and slowly picked up speed. The hardworking horse pushed the ratio of each gear to the dog's maximum RPM. One hour later, Denver had disappeared from the rearview mirrors.

"Don't you ever look at the map anymore to see how to get where you are going?"

"It seems like I've always got my head stuck in a map, but the trick is to remember which large cities you're going to go through and just follow the signs, from Denver to Kansas City to St. Louis, and from Louisville to Lexington to Winston Salem to Greensboro and then home. Having the signs directing you to the major cities always puts you on the best route to take, or at least that's the idea. But remember, these signs are not always there, so it's important to know the route to take."

Three hours more went by and the large, open land of Kansas was underfoot. The sun had peaked at its hottest point of ninety-four degrees and seemed to be maintaining a visible force field. When you were at the right angle and looked over the asphalt you could see the heat wave rising. It was too hot to put your arm in the window, but too uncomfortable not to have the air circulating around the body. This was a constant decision, and sometimes a sunburned arm would go in the window and sometimes not. The clean, quiet fragrance of open fields, an occasional silo, and a water tower or farmhouse dominated the land.

After a quick stop to take care of processed liquid, Jim relinquished the steering wheel to Shylo. It felt equally good to be able to stick that un-burned arm out the window. Shylo could tell the difference in driving the fully loaded unit. You could feel this difference by just riding in it, but even more so by driving it. Under a pull, the natural vibration in the steering wheel and gearshift was stronger, and the exhaust made a deeper, louder noise. The fuel pedal, which was pressed to the floor most of the time anyway, was now held on the floor more often. The brakes were more sluggish and required more space to stop. But driving the large vehicle was still and always an enjoyable thrill.

With both hands on the steering wheel, he said, "It's amazing how much heavier the twenty-five hundred pounds makes us feel. You would think we had put on ten thousand pounds the way this thing is pulling."

With a puzzled grin, Jim spoke, "Didn't it drive like that the other day when we were this heavy?"

"Yeah, but the other day I really wasn't sure if it was supposed to be that way or not."

"Oh, okay. That makes sense."

The day pressed on, and the steady noise of the vehicle tried to put you asleep, but the brilliant sun and its heat would not allow it. Hunger finally beat out the heat, and they stopped to eat. Afterward, Jim took the wheel.

"I hope we can sleep tonight. Nowhere in the United States do they have crickets that are as noisy as in Kansas."

One hundred and fifty miles away from Kansas City, he pulled off the road and selected a high spot to park. After getting out, he rolled the landing gear down. "I know I probably don't need to do this. When it's clear we sleep out in the open, but if it should rain, the trailer is full and we can't get inside."

"I never argue with 'the man'!"

"I'm your dad, slick, not 'the man'!"

Shylo grinned and made a small "X" with his finger, like he was writing on a chalkboard.

Jim pulled the lever that unlocked the dogs inside the fifth wheel and moved the tractor forward until the fifth wheel was at the end of the front of the trailer. On a drop frame trailer, one with a deck for the tractor wheels and a belly that is almost as low to the ground as a car, this made plenty of room to sleep under the deck if you put your feet underneath the belly. The view of the pin on the trailer was not like looking at the stars, but you would stay dry if it rained.

They went to the side door that contained furniture pad blankets, fresh clothes and toothbrushes. Shylo looked up quickly when Jim opened the door. A large sheet of plywood had been loaded against the wall above the large wood box. He knew the plywood was there and would hold everything in, but he couldn't help but flinch at what would fall out if it wasn't.

"That plywood works pretty good, doesn't it?"

Jim contained his grin and paid no attention before he spoke.

"Thirteen hundred miles. We'll be home Thursday afternoon." The deductive reasoning clicked inside Shylo's head. You should be able to do five hundred miles with ten hours of driving. A driver's logbook was scheduled for no more than ten hours of work for six consecutive days and then one full day off.

CHAPTER ELEVEN

At four p.m. on Thursday afternoon they rounded the turn on the dirt road six hundred feet away from their driveway. Jim was stretching hard to see over the bushes. The driveway was empty, which meant his stuff wasn't stacked up in the middle of it. His grin remained a smile as he stopped in front of the house and viewed Joyce standing on the porch. He jumped out and ran around the front of the truck to greet his darling, sexy wife. She bolted across the lawn. He was running, but slowly came to a stop and watched Shylo jump into his mother's arms. He remained holding his arms out to be next. She twirled around and kissed her son on the forehead twice before sitting him down. "You have no idea how I have missed you. I bet you've grown a half-inch!"

They started walking to the front door. With his arms still held halfway out, and a smile that was now half a frown, he yelled, "Where's Cannon?"

Without looking back, she yelled, "Swimming. He should be back in about an hour."

1965
oDessa, texas

CHAPTER ONE

In early October 1965, on a Saturday morning, Jim was taking Shylo to his new job. They walked into the offices of the thirty-five hundred square foot warehouse known in Odessa, Texas, as Best Way Moving and Storage. Jim proceeded around the counter to one of the smaller offices that surrounded the central office. He knocked on the door frame with an open door before entering.

"Good morning, Mr. Roy, how are you this morning?" Shylo looked at the sign on the open door that said "President," and followed his dad into the room.

A deep, friendly voice greeted them. "Well, good morning, Mr. Jim. I'm doing fine, and how about you?"

"Great, I brought my oldest son in to see the warehouse."

Shylo stood looking at the large painting on the wall. An old miner in wornout clothes was leading a pack mule through the desert. Most offices had distinguished pictures of national heritage or something impressive associated with their business, but this guy exhibited a picture of a bearded person who looked like he was on his last leg and about to die of thirst in the blazing sun. *Oh well,* he thought, *I guess it takes all kinds.*

"Shylo." He turned his head sharply toward Jim.

"This is my son, Shylo Desmond, and this is my boss, Roy Matthew."

"It's a pleasure to meet such a fine-looking young man."

Shylo looked over the desk at the balding person in a blue shirt and tie, and reached over to shake his hand. "It's a pleasure to meet you too, sir."

"Shylo worked for me for over three summers. Not only can he load the trailer, but he can also drive the truck as well as I can. He's fifteen, and in North Carolina he had a learner's permit, but here he's going to have to wait a few months until he turns sixteen and gets a regular Texas driver's license."

"Of course, he can't drive the big trucks here until after he's twenty-one and properly licensed, but after he's sixteen, maybe he can drive our pack truck. Otherwise, he can work extra for you when he's not going to school and you can use him. That way he can make some spending money."

"That would be absolutely great, sir. Not only can he load, but he can pack cartons too. In fact, when it comes to working, he knows a fair amount about everything in the business. And what makes him so great is that he's dependable."

Roy displayed half a smile and leaned back in his chair. "I wish all our employees had that quality. If Jacob Harrison doesn't show up for that El Paso job, I swear I'm going to fire him."

For five years he had been threatening to fire old Jake for not showing up to work. But he couldn't fire Jake without firing his entire crew of six men, because they were all guilty. Jake had the most experience, and therefore was the most depended upon.

Jim stood there in his new white shirt and black tie.

"Now, sir, let me handle it. After all, that's what you hired me for. If Jake doesn't show up, I've got Alfred Almond who said he'd go."

"But Jake usually drinks with Al. Who was going to help Jake?"

"Al."

"Then who would be Al's helper?"

"He said he had a relative who had no experience but was a hard worker and there would be no problem taking him. If I was a betting man I would bet they plan to take him anyway, add his hours on to theirs and pay him accordingly. But I wouldn't say anything to them, because if it should turn out to go over five thousand pounds they would have the extra help needed. Pack it tomorrow, load it Monday and drive back Tuesday. El Paso being three hundred miles from Odessa will make for three easy days for five thousand pounds."

Roy locked his fingers together and put his hands behind his head. "For Jake's sake there better be somebody in El Paso tomorrow to handle that shipment. If he cost me my largest account, in fact my only large account, I'll fire him for sure."

El Paso Tool and Dye was a large distributor of oil field equipment. Best

Way came across their business nine months earlier when Roy convinced the new division manager, Bryon Styles, to use his company to move a small section of their offices to Odessa, Texas. Even though he didn't drive a truck, Roy organized and handled the move. He impressed Bryon so much that Bryon put in a good word with the purchasing agent, and Best Way, with Red Horse as its prime carrier, ended up getting all of the company's moving business. Not only was Best Way handling all of their local business, but they also received the booking commission for all the long-distance work that Red Horse was hauling for El Paso Tool and Dye.

"I'm going to show Shylo the warehouse. Maybe I'll get him to hook up Jake's tractor and trailer, since it was never done."

"He can do that?"

"Oh yeah, he knows how to do it."

After entering the warehouse they looked at the two hundred foot crates stacked three high and three deep. All were in neatly organized rows. They contained household good shipments in storage. The wood containers could be loaded by forklift on a drop frame flatbed trailer and then used to pick up shipments or deliver out. In the back of the warehouse was a room for packing material and new cardboard boxes, and adjacent to this was a saw room. It contained a swing arm saw on a continuous cutting table. This was used for building crates for shipping plate glass, marble or whatever the delicate need be.

Standing in the saw room, Shylo looked up at Jim. "You think Jake will show up?"

"Maybe, at least I hope so."

"You need to hire people that are dependable."

"The crew here is no different than at any other moving company. It's a hardcore, backbreaking, thankless way to make a living. But any uneducated, air head can do it as long as he's willing to try. Once you realize it's your occupation or station in life, it tends to make most people drink. I'm sorry. I don't mean to have such a negative attitude, but what I just said is a fact of life. So don't pass judgment on these people, which I'm one of. Just remember how important your education is and the commitment to a realistic goal that will permit you to walk above ground and not get sucked into one of the potholes of life. Okay?" Shylo nodded his head yes and looked at his father with pride—he knew how smart he really was.

Returning back to the front, Jim finally showed off his office. Unfolding his arms and hands, he announced, "A desk with a phone sure beats out a steering wheel with a gearshift. The scenery doesn't change much, but I get to go home every night."

Shylo walked around the meagerly furnished but nice room. The desk and chair didn't match, but the chair had arms and casters and it swivelled. The center of the desk held an open daily dispatch book. To the right was a telephone and to the left a picture of Joyce, Cannon and Shylo. A straight-back, upholstered armchair was next to the desk. The left wall displayed two gray metal file cabinets and a large bookcase with a variety of books and office supplies.

The right wall held a large poster of the United States. Behind the desk was a window that faced out front. Jim shut the door, sat in the desk chair, leaned back and asked, "Do you think your mom's going to be okay here?"

"Oh yeah, Mom would be okay anywhere!"

Jim locked his fingers together, put his hands behind his head and looked at his desk. "I don't know, son. I had to talk like a stripped monkey to get her to move." Shylo sat up in the chair while he talked. "She wouldn't even listen until I convinced her that I wasn't going to be a driver anymore, that I would be a boss. It's been a major culture shock for her, and I know how hard it is to leave a place and start all over in a new one. Every night I try to convince her how great it is here, but the truth is that the grass isn't all that green. If we lose that El Paso account this place wouldn't need me. I don't know what the old manager did for so long before that account, but my job depends upon it. And all it would take would be one wrong word to lose it. And with so many people talking, sooner or later that word will pop up. We'll lose the account and I'll be out the door. I'm not trying to lay my problems on you, I just want you to know what's going on. I think you're that big now."

Shylo looked at Jim and smiled with an understanding look. "Why don't you go out in the main office to the keyboard, get the keys for tractor 301 and hook it up to trailer number 10. Use the side door in the coffee room."

He stepped out the side door into the yard. It was nine-thirty in the morning and the day was already starting to get hot. He thought to himself, *If only for a moment, I'll still get to sit behind the wheel of a truck.* He spotted two tractors without sleepers. They looked just like the one Jim drove, International Loadstars, except these trucks were way more hammered.

As he got closer, the dull, red paint, scratches and dents looked worse. He raised the driver's side hood on 301 and checked the oil. Not only was it up, but also it looked new. Lowering the hood, he twisted the handle back to the right to secure it.

Looking around the lot he spotted trailer number ten, backed up to an overhanging door at the end of the warehouse, where someone had loaded it with the packing material for the El Paso job. It was an older, round-nosed, twenty-five foot drop frame with a manual gate on the back. But it still looked very presentable with the large red stallion painted on each side. He climbed in and started the motor. The air gauge slowly rose to sixty pounds; patiently he waited until the needle stopped moving at just over a hundred and ten pounds. Then he got out, reached underneath the air tank and turned the cockpit valve a quarter turn. A defiant hissing sound broke the air, while a very murky-looking, gray substance was sprayed on the ground.

"Wow, I wonder if this thing has ever been bled." When the hiss turned to a weak noise of straight air, he turned the valve off and got back in. The air gauge was climbing from ten pounds. Again, he gave the motor some gas to help the compressor build up air. When the needle went just above sixty, he released the tractor brakes and pulled over to back underneath the trailer. Lining the drive wheels up with the inside of the trailer through the rearview mirrors, he backed up until the fifth wheel was underneath the deck. Stopping, he set the tractor brake, got out and climbed over the gas tank onto the frame behind the tractor. He disconnected the glad hands and electrical line from the attaching plate on the back of the truck. Unwrapping the lines from around the pogo stick, he spoke to himself, "All we had was a long, stretchable spring attached to the top center of the truck's back to keep the rubber lines up out of the drive line."

Taking one of the glad hands, he spit in the center of its rubber grommet so it would slide on easier and locked it on an exposed glad hand on the trailer. Repeating this process, he connected the other one and thought, *It sure would be nice if they had these things color coded, red to red and blue to blue.* Lifting the little spring-loaded door in the center above these connections, he pushed the electric pigtail in until the lever on top locked with the lever on the door. Then he climbed back in the tractor to operate the brakes. With no air in the trailer's system, the brakes will release and you can push the trailer back into something. With air in the system, the brakes will set up when the valve is set. He looked at the center of the dashboard. The valve for the trailer was different than the push-pull one for the tractor. It was a good-sized flat toggle switch that operated from left to right. Around it was a circular metal label that was two inches wide and said "Trailer Only."

With the motor still running, he flipped the toggle switch to the right. The gage held steady at one hundred and ten. He announced to himself, "Fifty percent chance of being right, and I'm wrong, of course!" He flipped the valve back to the left; got out and switched air lines. Climbing back in, he flipped it again to the right. The needle plummeted and a few seconds later came the familiar spurt of air from the brakes releasing. The needle stopped immediately and started to rise from seventy-five pounds. He got out and went to the back of the trailer. Looking underneath first, he crawled under and opened the valve to the air reservoir. Again, a very murky gray substance sprayed the ground. With the tank clear, he shut the valve, got back in the tractor and finished backing up until the trailer pin stopped the truck. Then he tried to pull forward, but the trailer held steady. This meant the fifth wheel was locked. He got out and rolled up the landing gear from the passenger's side.

Looking for a place in the yard to park the unit just so he could move it, he could see there was no designated place for vehicles. It needed to just sit right there. So he turned the motor off, retrieved the keys and headed back to his dad's office. Halfway alongside the warehouse he could smell the sweet odor of lilacs, but when he looked around he couldn't see so much as a weed, let alone a flower or lilac bush.

Stepping back into Jim's office he spotted two black men. One was very short and the other extremely tall, but both were wearing blue pants and white shirt uniforms.

Jim looked Shylo's way. "Did you get that taken care of?"

"Yes, sir, it's all ready except for checking the lights and bumping the tires."

"Gentlemen, I'd like for you to meet my son. Mr. Jacob and Mr. Alfred, this is Shylo."

Both men turned to greet him. Jacob grinned from ear to ear, exposing a mouth of very crooked teeth. He grabbed Shylo's hand with both his hands, shook it vigorously and said, "Just call me Jake."

With a straight face, Alfred reached out to shake hands and simply said, "Al."

"Shylo is going to work here part time, when we need him. He's a very good hand."

Jake coughed and spoke up. "That's good, that's good, Mr. Jim. We can sure use some good hands round here. Sometimes it seems like the only hands around here are the ones shaking a finger at yah." Jim looked at Jake, grinned and thought, *I bet Jake has threatened to quit more times than Roy has said he was going to fire him.*

60

"I's hate to break up good talkin', but if we's goin' to get there early enough to bed down, we better get to truckin'," said Jake.

"You got your expense money, paperwork and pens?"

Jake smiled and replied, "Yes, sir. Yes, sir. And yes, sir."

Remember, if you have any trouble before Monday morning, give me a call at home. You sure look sharp in those new uniforms. Have a safe trip."

"Yes, sir." And they left.

A few moments later Shylo replied, "They sure seem like good guys."

"They are." He looked up from his paperwork. "We have another part-time employee working here who's a year younger than you. Bill Styles, Byron's son, the manager for El Paso's Odessa division. Every chance we get I'm going to let you two work together. You can teach and watch out for him, okay?"

"Sounds good to me."

At that moment a noise came from outside that sounded like two cars colliding. Jim looked out his window while Roy went running by his door. Jim and Shylo followed. The three ran out the side door, into the lot. The front of trailer number ten was on the ground, and the tractor was a few feet in front of it. Jake and Al were standing there looking at the trailer.

While running up, Roy and Jim asked if they were okay. Jake looked under the trailer. It looked okay, then at the front of it the air lines had popped off and the electric wiring was pulled out of the pigtail. All in all, everything looked all right. Roy asked again if they were okay.

Jake started to shake his head from side to side and laugh. "It's a good thing it was empty. If it had been loaded, the landing gear would have gone up through the floor. As it is, it just bounced off the asphalt." He continued laughing and shaking his head while he looked at Shylo. Jim looked at Shylo with his head tilted back.

Jake walked up to Shylo, still laughing, and put his hand on his shoulder. "After you back the tractor underneath the trailer and try to pull it forward, the first thing you do is get out and look between the fifth wheel and trailer. If it isn't flat against it, or you can see light on one side, then the the fifth wheel is on a bind. When you raise the landing gear it unlocks them. So when you pull forward, the front of the trailer falls down. Fortunately, it looks like there was no damage."

He took his hand off Shylo's shoulder and looked at Jim, "If we can get the forklift out here and lift the front of the trailer and roll the landing gear down, I'll reconnect the pigtail."

Jim answered, "I'll get the forklift right now."

Jake's laugh was now a big smile. He retrieved the pigtail sticking out of the front of the van and went to the wiring harness hanging behind the drive wheels. He took a large knife from his pants pocket.

Roy walked up next to him. The sharp, four-inch tongue clicked when it popped out of the handle, and he held the switchblade pointing up. Roy backed off immediately, and Jake acted unaware. He used the blade to undo the small screw that held the two halves of the six-inch long, one-and-a-half-inch diameter metal pigtail together. One side contained five labeled brass screws for the wiring. The other side fit over it.

Jim came out with the forklift and lifted up on the front of the trailer while Al rolled the landing gear back down. Everyone ended up watching Jake rewire the pigtail. The lights and air lines checked out once the tractor was reconnected.

Jake and Al once again said goodbye. As Jake pulled away, he reported, "We'll see you sometime Tuesday!"

Jim replied, "I'll get the gate!"

Roy said on his way back inside, "Let's see if we can get out of here around noon."

Jim answered, "Sounds good to me." An hour later the three went home.

CHAPTER TWO

The move in late August had been a major change for the Desmond family. The open ranch country of Odessa was a radical culture switch from the heavily populated pine tree land of cotton and tobacco farmers around Fayetteville. Except for a little deeper Southern drawl and cowboy hats, the people in Texas were much the same. Neighbors knew neighbors, and gossip had a way of spreading like wildfire. And no matter what the story, it always seemed to start with the same words: "Don't tell anyone, but..."

Joyce's attitude was that she was, is and always would be unhappy about the transfer. But the excitement and satisfaction of Jim's new position, and Jim's almost-new company car, made the sacrifice bearable.

So far the change in public school systems seemed to be a novelty for the two boys. Their clothes seemed to be more polyester than the traditional Texas Levi's, and the shoes were loafers instead of the heavy duty looking cowboy boots. It wasn't uncommon to see boots on the girls. Even though cowboy hats were not allowed in school, every boy seemed to have a nice, dark, ten-gallon hat for dress, and a smaller, lighter colored version for work. At the beginning, this difference in apparel made them feel out of place, until it became apparent that sooner or later everyone wore their own style of clothing. Shylo was now in his second year of the high school system, and Cannon was in the seventh grade and still learning the more important basic knowledge of an education.

Shylo was now in a different world from his little brother: the world of racing hormones. They were always there, but somewhere, somehow, during that time they graduated from the boxcar derby to Formula One racing. Weekday mornings now meant that not a hair was out of place.

Cannon did not see or notice this metabolic change that he would imitate in just a few short years. His weekday still consisted of one teacher all day, from nine a.m. to three p.m., with a lunch and two play periods at Permian Grade School. Living just four blocks away from the school, he was always able to walk, weather permitting.

Shylo's weekday started at eight-thirty a.m. and went until three-thirty p.m. He had five different classes and teachers with a one-hour lunch, and then a one-hour study period at Lincoln High. His school was six blocks away in the opposite direction, so it took a little longer to walk each morning. Joyce would take him in the morning, but if she wasn't there in the afternoon he could walk home. He hated the waiting and walking, and vowed that he would work in the summer and make enough money to buy a car. Even when Joyce dropped him off or picked him up he felt like everyone was watching, and it was embarrassing for someone who had a learner's permit.

The school classes themselves were not too bad. He had algebra, English, history, science and P.E. Lunch was held in two periods, from eleven-thirty to twelve-thirty, and then from twelve-thirty to one-thirty. You always had time to do something after you ate, and the study period in the afternoon would give you time to do homework.

As usual, friends were hard to come by, but girls were impossible to figure out or understand. They went to all this extra effort to turn a boy's head, but then acted shy if boys took a peek. Gun shy or not, some of them would turn your head no matter what, especially the well-manicured blonde in algebra, or the girl with the long brown hair who always sat next to the windows in study period. The blonde was Carol, and the brown-haired girl was Daisy. He felt like he might forget his own name, but he could never forget theirs.

CHapTer THree

Late Friday evening, almost two weeks after Jake had dropped the trailer, the embarrassing memory of it was still etched strong in Shylo's mind. Even though everyone else had forgotten about it, it still plagued his thoughts at night.

The sound of a soft whistle drifted through the air, carrying the delicious smell of Joyce's pressure-cooked roast. Joyce was at the counter, mashing potatoes with a mixer to go with the gravy and string beans. Shylo and Cannon were sitting at the table, visiting with Mom. What they were really doing was waiting—waiting for Joyce's indescribably delicious home cooking. It was six-thirty p.m., and Jim was an hour late. Setting the table with plates, utensils and paper napkins, she announced, "If he's not here in fifteen minutes, we'll dig in without him." The boys looked at the clock. She spread a towel on the counter and retrieved a tray of Pillsbury butter biscuits from the oven. Carefully, they were put on the towel to cool.

"Shylo, get everyone a glass of tea while I finish."

Jim walked into the kitchen with his nose in the air. "You know, I could smell that roast up the street! I bet it's driving our neighbors insane."

Joyce looked at him with approval. "Well, I'm glad you could find your way to join us."

He kissed his smiling wife on her face and whispered, "Later, baby, later."

He stepped into the bathroom to wash up.

Returning, the table was set and all were waiting. He sat down and bowed his head, and everyone bowed their heads. He thanked God for his beautiful family and the food they were about to receive. Everyone said amen, and they started to eat. Taking the large fork and knife, he started cutting the meat.

"I don't know what smells best, the roast or the biscuits. You don't really need a knife to cut the meat; it just falls apart with the fork."

"Well, it had long enough to cook."

"I didn't think I was going to make it home this early. I think our pre-Christmas work has started. No matter where you are there always seems to be a thirty-day busy season right around Thanksgiving that will end as abruptly as it started."

He looked over at Shylo. "What are you doing tomorrow, Shylo?"

Concerned, Shylo looked up from his plate and said, "Oh, this must be an honor! You never call me by my first name!"

Jim grinned. "It slipped. How would you like to work tomorrow? I got three thousand pounds to pack and load. Sam Alright and Tony Novak will be delivering out forty-five hundred. If you and Bill could pack and inventory the three thousand, Sam and Tony can swing by when they're through, and the four of you could load it."

"Sounds good to me. How much do I make an hour?"

"The same as when you worked for me—a dollar and twenty-five cents an hour. Okay?"

"Okay."

"Good. This will give you a chance to meet Bill and work with him. He's a good boy, he just doesn't know anything about moving."

CHapTer Four

The next morning at seven, Jim and Shylo arrived at work, and within a few minutes all employees showed up plus one temporary laborer and Al's cousin, Trevor Wood. Full-time workers at Best Way consisted of two black drivers, Jacob Harrison and Alfred Almond, one black helper, Henry Topaz, one white driver, Sam Albright, and two white helpers, Tony Novak and Arnold Semon. No matter what the seniority, drivers worked first, but this was pretty much how it was done in all moving companies.

Jim stacked up the clipboards loaded with paperwork before going out in the main office to distribute them. Shylo stood in front of his desk and coughed to get his attention.

"Uh, if Bill is fifteen, who's gonna drive."

"Oh, I'm sorry; I forgot to tell you. You are. I already talked it over with Roy, and you'll only be going a few miles in the pick-up site. There is just nobody else, so if it's all right with you, I would sure appreciate it."

"Of course, I'll be careful."

"Good. It's already loaded with packing material and ready to go." Jim picked up the four clipboards, and they went out in the central office.

Shylo spotted Bill standing in front of the counter. He was a young man with a medium build in new black high tops; jeans; a lightweight, dark blue jacket; and a paisley print shirt. Jim stepped behind the counter and started talking.

"First of all, everything is loaded, fueled and ready to go. I won't try to fool you, it's going to be a long day, so the earlier we get started the earlier we'll get done. Al, Trevor and Jack from temporary labor will deliver out the ninety-five hundred to Midland on 301." He handed Al the top clipboard with keys. "Jake, Henry and Arnold will load the ten thousand they packed yesterday on 402." He handed Jake the second clipboard with keys.

"Sam and Tony will deliver out the forty-five hundred on the bobtail to Penwell, and then come back into Odessa to pick up the three thousand that Shylo and Bill are going to pack and inventory this morning." He handed the third clipboard and keys to Sam, the forth and final one to Shylo, and then he introduced Bill to everyone and asked, "Are there any questions? I know, as experienced as you guys are, I'm the only one who needs to ask the questions. Anyway, I'll be in and out of the office all day. If you need anything, call. If I'm not here, I'll be back in a little while." He looked at the clock hanging on the wall. It read seven-thirty-five a.m.

"So, if you want to all get after it right now, you can sign in at seven."

Everyone filled in the time on their time cards hanging next to the counter and filed out through the coffee room. Jim stopped Shylo. "Do you know where this address is?"

"No, I've got no idea at all."

"Then we better find it on the map." They walked over to a street map of the Odessa area. Shylo drew a map on the clipboard. Jim looked at the two young men.

"I'll be by a little later to check on you guys. Okay?"

Bill replied, "Yes, sir!" They then walked out through the coffee room.

The truck was parked in back, next to the door for packing material. The three other crews were already out of sight. Bill looked up at Shylo as they walked alongside the building.

"What school do you go to?"

"Lincoln."

"That's what my dad said. I go there too, but I'm a freshman and you're a sophomore. After two months, I'm surprised we haven't seen each other."

"Well, we didn't know each other until today. There it is again, that odor. Can you tell me why it smells like lilacs right here?"

Bill grinned. "Does, doesn't it? You would think the odor would be gone by now. It's been there ever since last August."

"I take it there's a good story behind it."

"Oh yeah." They got in the pickup, and Bill continued. His grin widened as he revealed the history of an event in August. "It was a Monday morning last summer, and everyone had showed up for work but Jake. About ten in the morning we were all still in the warehouse, working. Jake's wife pulls into the lot in a big red convertible. She pulled straight through the lot and stopped in front of a trailer that was sitting on the dirt. She started cussing and screaming at the trailer. For a while there we thought she had lost her marbles, then Jake comes running around the trailer for the warehouse. He looked like he was still about half drunk and couldn't move too fast. She backed up and took off on a dead run for him."

Bill laughed and shook his head. "For a moment it looked like she was gonna crush him between the front of the car and the warehouse. Then she stopped, stood right up in the middle of her seat, reached down and got a tall bottle of cologne. She nailed him smack in the head with it. The bottle broke and knocked him down. He managed to get back up, dripping wet with perfume, and looked at her. She stood there holding on to the top of the windshield and yelled, 'You ever come on my place again and I'll put a hole in you big enough to shit through!' I'll tell you what, if she ever yelled at me to stand at attention my head would go straight in the air and my arms would go stiff at my sides. Anyway, Al brought his car in the lot, loaded Jake inside, went to the back of the trailer he was in, got a girl out, put her in the back seat and left. A little while later he came back with an empty car and went back to work. Except for Roy telling me to clean up the glass alongside the building, there was no more said about it."

Shylo was laughing at the obscurity of Jake's dilemma. "How did she know where he was at, or even what trailer he was in?"

"I have no idea, but when he didn't show up for work the next day everyone figured he wouldn't be back. But bright and early Wednesday morning he was there, howdy-doin' everyone with that great big ol' grin like things just couldn't be better. You felt more like patting him on the back instead of just saying howdy."

"Look for Mervin Street and then we turn right."

"Okay. How long you been doing this?"

"Just in the summertime for a few years; it feels good to be making money again."

"Yeah, I know what you mean."

Shylo turned on Mervin Street and asked, "How long have you been working for Best Way?"

"Only since last summer, and then part time after school started. I know you know who my dad is, and it's no big deal, but this job is still better than working at a hamburger place or being a janitor at Dad's work."

"What period do you have lunch at school?"

"The first period."

"Me too. We'll have to get together sometime and eat."

"I generally have the school lunch in the cafeteria."

"Me too. I'm surprised one of us doesn't remember seeing the other, but it is a big place."

Shylo parked in front of the duplex they were looking for. "Well, let's go see if Mr. Brimestead is ready for this!" He pushed the doorbell, and stood holding the clipboard. A casually dressed young man opened the door.

"Mr. Brimestead, are you ready to move?"

He pointed toward the street. "You're not going to try and put it in that little pickup, are you?"

They laughed at the funny remark until they realized he was serious. Shylo replied, "No, sir, we are going to pack and get it ready. We have a big truck coming in a little while to load it."

"Good, come in and let me show you what I have. It's not much, only three rooms and a bathroom."

Four hours later they sat at the kitchen table, eating the hamburgers Mr. Brimestead had gotten for them. Everything was packed and inventoried, and he had already left the scene. The doorbell rang, and Shylo answered it while still eating.

Jim stood in the door. "Just what I like to see, a hungry person chowing down."

"The shipper got us the lunch. He signed the paperwork and left already. Everything is ready except for taking the legs off the kitchen table, and we'll do that in a minute."

Jim surveyed the three rooms—kitchen, living room and bed room, and smiled.

"They should be here any minute, and you'll be able to blow it on. Come back to the warehouse and unload it. We need that bobtail real bad the first thing Monday." Jim looked at Bill, who had been silent. "How's it going, Bill? This guy isn't working you too hard, is he?"

"No, sir, I'm just enjoying this tasty lunch!"

"Good. If you guys are okay then I'll see you back at the warehouse."

CHAPTER FIVE

At first period lunch on Monday, Shylo spied Bill at a table. He took his tray of food and joined him.

Bill looked up as he sat down on the other side of the table. "Hey, my main man; how's it going, stud?"

"Stud! Stud! Do you know where I can corner any fillies at?"

"Well, if I did I wouldn't tell you. I'd put them in my own corral."

They both laughed and continued with lunch. Shylo opened his milk. "They give you these little cartons of milk that wouldn't fill a glass. Just once I'd like to see them handing out a soft drink of our choice."

"I'll settle for the milk. If you complained they would probably just feed you water. At least we got eight hours in Saturday to earn spending money, right?"

"Oh, not for me. All my money goes in a sock. By the end of this summer I'm going to have both a driver's license and a car. Next year I'll come to school in style."

"Really? What kind of a car are you gonna get?"

"Well, I got my eye on that new sixty-two Corvette, but I got a funny feeling I'm gonna have to settle for less."

"I've seen that car. We're talking hot! But you would have to knock over two banks and the general grocery store to afford it. And then they wouldn't let you drive it to school because everyone would be out in the parking lot looking at it."

"Well, don't worry. It won't happen, but I can dream."

They finished their meal and eyed the opposite sex at other tables. Generally, the best looking ones did not eat in the cafeteria. They always had something more exciting planned that only involved a small bag of potato chips. Or they were fortunate enough to have access to a vehicle and could drive or ride to get a hamburger.

Shylo asked, "Is the weather always this radical around here? It went from eighty-five Saturday to fifty-five on Sunday. It's noon now, and you could still flip a coin as to which way it will go."

"Indian summers are always that way around here, but before Christmas it will tend not to go over a high of fifty-five." They both sat there in short-sleeved shirts. You would have to be a real nerd not to leave your coat in the locker during school hours, no matter what the temperature outside was.

Bill asked, "You wanna go in the gym and watch the girls' P.E. class practice for cheerleaders?"

Shylo smiled as the suggestion broke the boredom. "I didn't know you could do that. Sounds good to me."

"Let's get rid of these trays and go."

CHAPTER SIX

The holidays rolled in with all the tradition and vigor of old. At Thanksgiving dinner, Joyce stated, "Did you know turkey has a natural sedative that makes you want to sleep?"

Jim replied, "If I didn't hear that at least once during the meal it wouldn't be Thanksgiving!"

Christmas was now a time to keep mouths shut, for Cannon's sake. And Cannon wasn't about to open his mouth, because those who didn't believe didn't receive. For a few days the smell of pine trees and mint dominated the air, and the excellent taste of eggnog, homemade fudge and peanut butter balls intrigued the tastebuds. Shylo and Bill had since received a pair of uniforms each. They were also included in the Christmas presents under the company tree, along with a cash bonus of twenty dollars. The presents that were all the same size turned out to be the dark blue uniform work jackets with a removable lining. Your first name, or nick name, was on the front left above the pocket. In the center of the back was a Red Horse semi with the famous stallion on the trailer. From its front corner the large, muscular body was standing firm. The small head was held high, and the wind was blowing through its heavy mane. They were both tempted to wear their jackets to school, but didn't. They would obliviously be identified as wearing their daddy's work coat, and this just wouldn't be cool.

New Years popped up and back down, creating a reason for everyone to decide on new resolutions. Then, without so much as a goodbye, the holidays rolled out like a signification leaving the established days of winter.

A few hours of work managed to spring up each week, usually at the warehouse, but sometimes out on a job. Shylo continued teaching Bill the business. It was good to tell someone else how instead of somebody else telling you. A couple of times he even got to drive a tractor and trailer somewhere. Each time, Roy stated it would be the last, but when it comes to making a dollar, moving companies will do what has to be done. Bill, who looked up to Shylo anyway, thought this was beyond belief. When he helped him hook up a trailer or watched him back one up to a door, he would look with total admiration. More than once he told him the same thing.

"Other guys do flips just to drive the family car—you're out driving the company semi."

One time Shylo shook his head and grinned, saying, "But I don't ever go very far—really!"

Bill replied with an effort of high, tense emotion. "Yeah, but it's the idea that you can do it, and that you *do* do it;"

Shylo grinned and didn't say anything else. He wasn't trying to make light of Bill's admiration. He valued this very highly. He just didn't want him to make him something he wasn't. But after all was said and done, he knew he could drive a semi, so Bill must be right.

CHapTer seven

January ended and February took over. It was Saturday, and there was only one job on the books. A small twenty-five hundred pounds for delivery out was what had to be done. It had been loaded on a trailer behind 301. It was high noon, and Sam and Tony, who optioned to work, were a no-show. Nobody seemed available, but the shipment still had to be delivered. Shylo and Bill were in high demand.

Shylo had picked Bill up in Joyce's car, per Jim's instructions. The gate was closed, but the big padlock on the chain was not locked. Jim was out on a pre-move survey. The keys and paperwork were left in 301. Shylo started the truck and waited for sixty pounds on the air gauge. He pulled forward and stopped.

"The only thing we're gonna check is the inside of the trailer. It would be embarrassing to pull up to the residence with an empty trailer!" He checked the trailer and got back in. After looking at the small map on the paperwork, he pulled outside the gate.

"You want to shut and lock that gate, Bill?" A moment later Bill got back in, and Shylo announced, "Looks like we're gonna go right through Odessa. It shouldn't be very crowded today."

He pulled out, heading straight for town, both boys in their white uniform shirts, dark blue pants and dark blue work jackets. The closer they got to town, the narrower the streets got. Shylo made a right turn on Grant Avenue and really had to get close to the car waiting to turn left, so his trailer would clear the corner. The lady driving the car watched the large bumper coming within inches of her door.

Shylo looked in the car and announced to himself without speaking out loud, "Oh no, my English teacher."

She looked up quickly at the driver, and then back down at the bumper. Then her head jumped back up with larger eyes as she looked at Shylo. The bumper cleared the car, and the trailer wheels cleared the curb. He drove away with no desire to look back or even to tell Bill.

CHAPTER EIGHT

That Monday, Janice, the English teacher, observed Shylo as he walked in the classroom and sat down. For five minutes she looked at him with a blank face, until the class settled down. Shylo suspected she felt like she was responsible to do something, but she didn't have the least idea what. Then she called him up to the front. He reported, and stood at an imaginary attention.

She asked, "Do you have a twin brother?"

He grinned at this thought and replied, "No, ma'm." For a long moment she looked at him before telling him to sit down. Even after he sat down she continued to look with that blank stare. Then she turned her head to the left and back to dismiss whatever was on her mind. She never said anything about the incident, but for the rest of the year Shylo couldn't enter her class without getting a long, blank look from Janice.

CHAPTER NINE

The drudge days of education had taken a hard right turn for Shylo. The compulsive obsession of long-legged beauties with a variety of blossoming breasts, smiles and toppings made the day worth looking forward to. Every day from Monday to Friday your appearance had to be notably worthy or you just didn't make the grade. The illustrious population of girls at Lincoln High had been whittled down to a couple handfuls of desirable selections. But almost all remaining were still eligible to run the race. Daily, Bill and Shylo observed this category of looks, but did not approach the girls.

Then one day Bill walked up to Shylo in the hall. He was holding the hand of a cute little thing with long brown hair. He said, "Hi, this is Nancy. We have study period together." Shylo stuck his hand out, but they kept on walking by. He jerked his hand back and realized that in a crowded place that was not cool, and in a world of heavy competition you could not afford to not look cool.

For the rest of the school year, except for the occasional chance of sight (and he was always in the company of Nancy), Bill seemed to just disappear. The only time he re-appeared was during those few unpredictable hours of work each week. Shylo was not mad or even jealous; Bill just seemed to be winning the race that he started running first. Like the quick hesitation of vapor that is sprayed from a can, the articles of life move on. The days become warmer, the nights a little shorter, and the petals of God's flowers that open in the sunlight and close at twilight make known the arrival of spring.

CHAPTER TEN

It was the middle of April, and Jim's family had only been in Odessa for a little over seven months. Tuesday evening, Jim beckoned all of the family to sit at the dining room table. With everyone perched in a seat, he stood up like the chairman at a conference table.

Joyce grinned at him. "You need a small wood hammer to start the proceedings."

He grinned and replied, "A motion is set before the committee by Joyce. I should have a gavel. Those who approve of this motion can indicate 'yea' by raising your right hand."

Everyone's right hand went up, except for Joyce's. Both of her hands went up. "Now, everyone who disagrees with this motion, indicate nay by raising your hand." Nobody's hand went up. "That settles it, the motion is carried. I should have a gavel. Now, I have another motion to put before the board. We're not gonna vote on this one until our next meeting in a few days. Now, first of all, this information stays in this room. Do you understand, Cannon?"

"Yes, sir."

"How about you, Mr. Shylo?"

"Yes, sir."

He paused for a few moments and looked hard at his two boys to convey his sincerity. "Monday morning, the regional manager for Red Horse Van Lines, Mr. Joseph Johnson was in the office. There was a tense, closed-door meeting between him, Roy and Roy's wife, the secretary. I have strongly suspected a meeting of this nature, and it finally happened. Anyway, I'm gonna cut to the chase and deliver the bottom line. Best Way Moving is gonna have a slow season. They're gonna have to cut back their already meager work force. I have been given until the end of May. Like our customers with children, school will be out, and it will be easier for us to move. Since Roy paid for our move out here, he'll pay for our move back."

He grinned and lifted his eyebrows. "He'll move us anywhere in the United States, not including islands. Your Uncle Harry has been hard after me to come out to California and go into the grocery store business with him. Or we can go back to Fayetteville, North Carolina, and I will find work there. When we moved out here it was more or less my option to better myself, and I deeply appreciate your indulgence. Knowing the outcome, if I had it to do over again, I wouldn't, but I don't regret trying. This time everyone will have a say in the decision after a couple of days to think it over."

Joyce spoke up. "We already voted today, so let's go to California." Jim looked at her with a bewildered stare.

1966
california

CHAPTER ONE

Harry walked slowly as he showed Jim and Joyce the moderately stocked shelves of a small store in Olivehurst, California. Olivehurst was a very small military and migrant worker town in the northern part of Central California. It lay west of Beale Air Force Base, and a few miles south of Marysville. The small store was on the north end of the main street of town, next to the highway. The highway contained intermittent sections of freeway, with a cloverleaf for Olivehurst.

Harry and his wife, Martha Desmond, had a three-year-old son, Joey, and a two-year-old daughter, Crystal. Harry was a lifetime military person stationed at Beale AFB. He had been working part time at the well-to-do grocery store in the center of town. He had also been after Jim to start up a grocery store with him for some time. He lived in a trailer court in a three-bedroom trailer just four blocks away from the store. He said to Jim as they walked through the center of the store, "I've had my eye on this place for a long time."

A little old lady was at the front in the middle of the store, behind an antique-looking cash register. The small "For Sale" sign in the front window had been there for three years. The building was on a small incline with a wide sidewalk and a western-style front above the large plate glass windows on each side of the tall double front doors. The inside contained three double-sided display shelves in the center of the floor and a small walk-in freezer in the back. Mounted shelves were on the wall to the left as you came in the front door, and a glass meat bin and vegetable bin were on the right wall. The cash register was toward the front door, surrounded by a counter. A water-filled electric pop machine with two large, lightweight doors were beside the counter. Candy racks were to the right, behind the cash register.

A single door in the back led to the outside, straight into an old, rundown place that was a cross between a shack and a house. A dim trace of paint still existed in small areas on the wood, but when you chipped the paint off the wood underneath had that dark color of age.

The elderly lady behind the cash register lived in the apartment across the street. She opened the door only for potential buyers. With the new, modern, innovative convenient stores, this place needed to be taken down, contents and all. But Harry had the idea and knowledge to become as prosperous and successful as the store down the street.

Harry thanked the lady for her time and courtesy while the others walked out front, looked up and discussed the western-style face of the building. Then they left and went to Harry's trailer to sit at his table and talk. While they sat at the round kitchen table, Harry relayed his ideas.

"What we need to do is make this a family operation. Between the two families we should be able to keep the doors open from daybreak to dark. It will just take a few phone calls to start the vendors delivering again. I know it doesn't have much in it right now, but what we need to do is not take anything out of it. If Jim can find a full-time job to support his family, and we can keep the store open, we can put all of the store's profit back into the stock. If we do this, the place can't do anything but grow, and I have over twenty years of experience in this business from working part time at local grocery stores. I can answer almost any question that comes up!"

Two days later, Jim and Joyce rented a two-bedroom house, and the following day their furniture was delivered.

Another two days later Jim secured a job in Marysville, selling used cars.

Four days later, "Desmond's Market" was printed across the top front of the store.

On the first of June they opened the front door for business. A small credit book for Jim's family and one for Harry's family was started. The bill expected to be paid in full, no discounts or freebies—just the temporary credit. After all, you'd have to pay cash anywhere else.

An argument immediately arose about who would get to work the most hours. Then reality set in. If Jim and Harry worked full-time jobs, they had to have time to eat, sleep and bathe. Jim's job at the car lot was from noon until eight or nine p.m., Monday through Saturday. Harry's job at Beale AFB was from six a.m. until two p.m., Monday through Friday. Joyce and Martha could work various hours, but they still needed time to cook and keep house. Martha would need a babysitter. So it was decided she would only work one to two hours at a time when needed to fill in, and she would bring the children with her.

Shylo was the only candidate for a full-time, non-paying job, since Cannon was too young to be considered. He wondered what his part would be. Jim made a deal with him with everyone listening.

"If you'll give the store five and a half full days a week, 44 hours, then I'll make it worth your while before school starts.

Shylo grinned real big and said, "Okay."

His verbal contract with Jim was instantly forgotten, and quietly the dream of a 1962 Corvette flew out the window without bothering his attention. For the first few days until Sunday, everyone worked who could be there. Then the business was closed until Monday morning.

CHAPTER TWO

Sunday afternoon, after one of Joyce's famous baked pork chops and scalloped potato meals, the five knights of the Desmond Market surrounded the table. A work schedule had to be established and agreed upon. Until school started, Shylo's hours would be from seven a.m. to three p.m., Monday through Friday. Jim would give him a half-hour break from eleven a.m. to eleven-thirty a.m., before he went to work. Joyce would work from three p.m. to six p.m., and Harry would work from six p.m. to nine p.m. On Saturday, Jim would work from seven a.m. to eleven a.m. Shylo would go from eleven a.m. to three p.m., and Harry would take over from three p.m. to nine p.m. Martha would be used for fill in whenever anyone couldn't make it. Jim would spend more time allotted training the others, but work done in addition to the schedule was not considered a part of it. When the store hours or anyone's time frame changed, then the scheduled hours would be revised.

After this badly needed organizing session, everyone removed their elbows from the table and was served a goodly slice of Joyce's chocolate mousse cake. Chocolate ice cream was inside the cake. Short, slightly overweight Harry sat looking at the delectable dish.

"You know, if it was anything but this I would be too full to eat it, but…" He stopped talking and started to eat.

Jim started eating without hesitating. "Well, I was smart and saved room. By the way, honey, I love your cooking."

"I know, that's my problem. I love it too. But I'll tell you what, if I break that two hundred mark, we're going to go on a starvation diet." Jim, Martha and Harry stopped eating for a moment and looked up in dismay that she would give her weight away. She realized the error of her mistake and just continued to look at the center of the table.

Jim looked up a second time and realized she wasn't eating. "Aren't you gonna have any?"

"No."

He thought about it. If she dieted, there would be no more of her good cooking. "Good."

He finished his cake.

CHAPTER THREE

Monday morning, 8:01 a.m., and Jim set straight up in bed.

"We slept in."

Quickly, he rousted Shylo from bed. Cannon pulled the sheet over his head and realized there were advantages to being young. A moment later his disturbed slumber was forgotten, and he was asleep again.

Shylo struggled to get ready in two minutes and leave with Jim.

Ten minutes later their Pontiac Tempest station wagon slid up to the sidewalk in front of the store. The old lady across the street, who always seemed to wear the same black dress, grinned as she looked over her newspaper and out the window at father and son racing for the front door of the store. Jim looked at Shylo as he unlocked the front door.

"It's a good thing we don't have to answer to anyone, but this just will not work." The lock clicked, the door opened, and they went inside. "When you set the standards, it's imperative that you meet those obligations. In the future, we can't be turning the alarm off and going back to sleep. No harm done, though." He turned the closed sign to open on the front door. "We need to turn the overhead lights on."

Shylo took care of the lights while Jim opened the cash register and took out a small key. The florescent lights flickered and came on, brightening everything in the room. He unlocked the cabinet doors underneath the counter and retrieved the green metal cashbox from among the various bottles of wine.

"I feel like Dopey in the movie *Snow White*, when he locked the diamonds up in the shed and then put the key on a big nail next to the door." He raised the lid and distributed the cash to the appropriate slots in the till.

"Okay, boss, it's all yours. The meat man will be by later, and Harry's list of what we need is right here." He pointed at the slot and then shut the drawer.

"I'm gonna go down the street and get a paper. If I can talk your mom into fixing breakfast, I'll be back shortly and you can go eat. If not, then I'll be at home reading the paper."

He left, and Shylo sat on the wooden stool behind the counter. Everything had been dusted and cleaned, and the meat case had been made ready for some product. What the whole place needed was more product, but hopefully that would come in time. The entire morning went by with only one sale: a fifty-cent pack of cigarettes.

Jim came in asking, "Did you sell anything?"

"Yeah, twenty smokes."

"Don't worry, it's gonna get better. Your mom fixed that breakfast for lunch. There are eggs, sausage, biscuits and gravy, the whole nine yards. The keys are in the car."

"Sounds good to me."

"Make sure you're back here at eleven-thirty so I won't be late, okay."

"Yes, sir."

Just before eleven-thirty, Shylo returned. Jim sat on the stool, studying a small book.

"Wow, doesn't time fly when you're having fun."

"The keys are in the car."

He left, and Shylo was alone again. Then in walked a long-legged beauty. She was fifteen years old, with long brown hair, large brown eyes and a sexy figure that was hidden behind a pleated dress. She walked up to the counter and asked, "Do you have any cold Cokes?"

He pointed at the pop machine. She had been in it before, but acted like she hadn't.

"Fifteen cents includes the five-cent deposit on the bottle."

"Well, if I drink it here it will only cost me a dime, huh?"

"If you drink it here I'll pay for it." He took a dime out of his pocket and put it in the till.

One hour later (with two interruptions for the sale of cheap wine), they knew each other's history. Her name was Nancy Carter; her dad, Fred Carter, was stationed at Beale AFB. Her mother's name was Patty Carter, and her thirteen-year-old sister's name was Kathy Carter. She lived one block away, between the store and his house, and next year she was going to be a junior at Yuba High in Marysville, the same school he was destined to attend.

When Joyce walked in they were still talking over an empty bottle of Coke. She grinned real big at the sight of them and walked over.

He spoke up. "This is my mother, Joyce, and this is Nancy Carter."

"Looks like I better start worrying about my son."

"Her father is stationed at Beale AFB. She invited me to her house this Saturday to play croquet."

"Did the meat guy show up?"

"No."

"Good, I'd really rather Harry is here for that first time." She had walked behind the meat counter.

Shylo looked at Nancy. "Can I walk you home?"

"Yes."

"Mom?"

She peeked over the counter. "I'll see you later, bud. It was a pleasure to meet you, Nancy."

"The pleasure was all mine."

They went out the front door and down the side street on the west side of the building. He observed the rundown house behind the store. The front yard looked like it had never seen grass. The lesser part of a picket fence was around the front perimeter. It looked like the house never seen sunlight in the summertime because of five gigantic garbage trees, two in front and three in the back. The back served as host to about eight antique miscellaneous items hidden by the house and surrounding bushes. There was a rusted wringer-type washer and a badly decayed wooden ice box, among other things.

He asked, "Have you ever seen the people that live there?"

"Yes, a mother and her thirteen-year-old son, Emily and Mike Toon. The lady is a short person with a badly deformed right arm, but her son has got hair so red that you can't look at it when the sun is shining on it. My little sister says he's cute as a button. In fact, he's the first boy, the only boy, to ever kiss her, and she would choose him over John Lennon any old day."

He looked at her out of the corner of his eye with his head in the air. "Did you ever kiss him?"

"No! What do you think I am, a cradle robber?"

"No! No! I was just asking."

He looked at her again, like before, and asked, "If he did, would it be your first?"

Nancy turned in his direction, inhaled and exhaled sharply, then asked demandingly, "What are you doing, writing a book?"

"No! No! No harm meant. Just because one person rode the horse doesn't mean another person can't…" Then he shut up as he realized the enigma of his own words. She turned around and continued on. She looked more like she was stomping instead of walking. He followed, trying hard to think of something to say that would redeem him. "You'll hurt your ankles walking like that, and they are beautiful ankles!"

She ignored him, and he committed to keep his mouth shut.

At the end of the block they turned to the right. Halfway down the block she stopped in front of a nice single-level brick home to the left. It had a good-sized front porch with a swing, and sat in the middle of a third acre of green grass.

"This is home. Somebody lived here before we did, and someone will probably live here after we leave."

He pointed down the road with a weak arm. "I live at the end of the street, to the left, the first house on the right."

"I know where you live. Thanks for the Coke. Goodbye."

"Bye."

He looked down at the road as he finished walking home. He walked into the kitchen and sat at the table. Looking at the table but not seeing it, he thought, *My big mouth and me; I could ruin anything.* Then his prognostication changed. He looked at the little toy soldier lying on the floor and said out loud, "I don't know what she got so upset about. It would've been my first kiss."

Shylo then got up, walked through the living room, took a quick look at Cannon, who was busy with a steak knife, whittling a sharp arrow for his bow, and went into the bedroom to lie down for a nap. He went to sleep, shoes and all.

The next thing he knew, Joyce was pushing on his shoulder. "Hey, hey, love bunny, are you hungry or have you lost your appetite?"

He put his legs over the side of the bed and sat up. "I'm starved."

"Good, let's go in the kitchen and have a bologna sandwich before Cannon eats it all."

Like a drunken person, he stumbled behind his mom into the kitchen.

"Sit down and I'll get you a sandwich."

He looked at Cannon from across the table. "Hey, stranger, kill anyone today with an arrow?"

He stopped his fast chewing long enough to answer. "Not yet." He returned to his chomping like he was in a hurry.

The smell of bologna, lettuce, tomato and mayonnaise encircled the room. She set down the plate with a glass of Southern, sweetened ice tea and said, "If you get a few minutes, your uncle wants you to come to the store. He would like to show you a couple of things; it's nothing you have done wrong, just things he would like to show you. He says you're the main man, and he never gets to see you." She went around the corner, and back up to the counter. "What's Nancy like?"

Cannon's eyebrows went up as he looked at his older brother.

CHapter Four

By Thursday morning the schedule for the store was now a pattern. Shylo had discovered that a day of work was much better than sitting behind the counter, watching the front door. The meat counter now contained a metal tray of ground hamburger, a long roll of bologna and four other rolls of meat. The weight machine was on top of the display bin with a new dispenser rack of white butcher paper. A fresh pad of clear wax meat paper sat between the paper and weight machine. At the end of the bin was a wooden butcher block over a cabinet. It held the slicing machine for cutting bologna and other meats, and a stationary tape dispenser. The bread rack was stocked and was scheduled to be restocked every week. A bundle of the *Marysville Gazette* was sitting at the front door in the morning. It was untied and put in the display rack first thing.

Shylo was mechanically setting cans off the shelf and cleaning that area with soap and water. The small bell over the front door rang, and he returned to his spot behind the counter. A nice-looking young girl with short black hair was opening an orange drink at the bottle opener on the pop machine. She turned and set the dripping wet soda on the counter. Constantly moving her head and grinning, she acted as if she was afraid to meet his eyes.

He continued with business. "Fifteen cents, please."

She laid a dime and a nickel on the counter. "Hi, my name is Kathy." His head popped up when he recognized the name.

"Nancy wants to know if you're still coming over to play croquet this Saturday."

"I didn't know I was still invited."

She giggled, like she knew something he didn't. "Well, apparently so, or she wouldn't have talked me into coming down here to find out."

"What time? I work between eleven a.m. and three p.m."

"How about any time after work then?"

"Sounds good to me."

"Okay, we'll see you the day after tomorrow." Her dark eyes finally met his, she grinned even bigger, and her eyebrows flinched while she looked into his eyes. She picked up her drink and walked out the door. He took his towel from its nail under the counter and wiped up the water. He looked back at the door and thought, *I can't imagine a boy kissing her; she'd die from intense emotions.*

He returned to his shelf cleaning with a big smile. He opened the back door to get rid of the gross-looking water. A young redheaded boy was across the way.

"Hi, my name's Shylo."

"Hi, I'm Mike."

Stepping out the door, he dumped the water and set the pail down. Looking at the five metal garbage cans he asked, "When does the garbage run?"

"Tomorrow. I'll set them out for you."

He was going to say no, but he looked at how the cans were so close to their front door. There was no path or entryway to the back of the house. "Where do you keep your cans at?"

"We use one of those."

Shylo covered his grin for a moment and said, "I would be grateful if you would set them out."

"Do you guys give credit?"

"Give credit to whom?"

"To my mom."

"How would she pay?"

"She gets a check from the state every month."

"You need to come in the store in a little while, shortly after eleven, and talk to a guy named Jim. I'll let him know you're coming, okay?"

Mike turned and disappeared in the house.

Shylo took the bucket and went back in. He went to the small stock room to the left, just inside the door, and retrieved some clean water at a deep metal sink. This was the only sink in the building, and next to it was a small bathroom that only contained a toilet. You were required to wash your hands every time before handling the meat. The sink only had cold water, but at least it wasn't far away. He picked the bucket up out of the sink and returned to the shelves.

By the time Jim had walked in, he had done the entire side of a three-level display counter. He put the water in the stock room and reported to Jim. "The people in the back want to know if they can have credit. A young boy is going to come over and see you in a minute."

"Who's going to pay the bill?"

"His mother, who doesn't get out very much, but she receives a state check every month."

Jim took out a new credit book, like theirs, and wrote "State Check" on the back of it.

Underneath that he put an "X" by the three blank lines for information such as their weekly credit limit and the mother's Social Security number.

He attached the book to a small clipboard and put it under the counter. "When he comes over I'll have him take this back to his mom to fill out. There's good money in credit, if they pay their bill. Did we sell anything today?"

"Yep! We're starting to sell as much bread as we do wine. Are the keys in the car?"

Jim handed him the keys across the counter. "I got a bad habit of always taking them out. Next week they're going to let me use a demo car, so your mom can have this one. See you in a little bit." He sat on the stool, and Shylo left.

A few minutes later, and he was back. "Did he come over?"

"Yes, his mother filled out the book, and he returned it already." He opened the custom drawer under the cash register and took out the book. The cover was thin, sturdy cardboard with a front that folded back and slid under each new sheet with its copy. Three carbon sheets were supplied for the entire book. The front cover was filled out with the name and address. The back cover had the additional information. Jim explained how to use it.

"They have a thirty-five dollar a week limit, and all weeks go Monday through Saturday." Jim whispered the next part. "If these people go over, date it for the next week, but make sure you let them know. In fact, ask them if that's what they want to do. Always add the purchase up on the ten key. If it's only one item, then you just total up the one item. They get that receipt. You fill out the page in the credit book with the cardboard under the copy. The carbon goes between the pages, with the shiny side down. You enter every item purchased, the total, the date, the amount of credit left, and they sign it. Always ring the total amount of the purchase up on the cash register. It makes it official, and then give them the copy. Keep the original in the book. Always fill out a new page for a receipt. Mark the amount paid and how. If you cash a state check, mark the amount they get back. I told Mike we didn't have dairy products yet. He said they would just go up the street for that stuff. Any questions?"

He looked at Jim with uncertainty and apprehension. "I'm sure there will be."

"Well, let's take good care of these people. It's people like them that our business is dependant upon. It's people like them that will enable us to get that dairy cooler, and that's a must. The government is going to start a program to give away cheese. It's going to be given to everyone, but if you don't handle dairy products to begin with you're not going to be eligible to be a distributor."

He looked at the clock on the wall. "I have to go!" Shylo handed him the car keys, and he turned and headed for the door. "Have a good afternoon, and sell lots."

"Be careful, and don't kill any dumb people—smart people need them to do the work."

"That's a big ten-four, good buddy."

Fetching the bucket, he returned to the opposite half of the display counter and thought, *This side should be easier—it looks like there are less cans.*

He was going to start putting a section of canned goods down when someone came in for a pack of cigarettes. When he returned, he stood there with his hands on his hips and reasoned. This is good, but not absolutely necessary. He carried the bucket to the back, dumped the clean water in the sink and went back to the stool. After fifteen minutes of sitting there, watching the front door, he growled, went back and filled the bucket with soapy water and returned to his project.

One hour later, Mike, the redheaded boy, walked in carrying a list. He proceeded to put items on the counter from the list. After Shylo filled his order for hamburger, bologna and ham, he watched as Mike brought the items to the counter. He couldn't help but feel sorry for anyone whose main diet was from a store so small it didn't have a shopping cart. He finished, put the list in his pocket and stood in front of the counter.

"She needs a carton of Winston."

Uh-oh, this was the first time a minor had tried buying cigarettes for an adult, and this was a problem.

"She needs the cigarettes, or you need them?"

"She needs them."

Shylo's concern was to do the right thing, legal or not. "I tell you what, after everything is bagged, I'll look out front to make sure no one's coming, lock the front door and help you carry everything home. Okay?"

With one finger, he slowly entered the cost of each item on the ten key. Then, in small print, he put everything in the credit book. After a few minutes of mentally exhausting work, he had Mike sign it. He gave him the copy, and the receipt he had taken from the ten key. "Give these to your mom; they both have the sales tax and the total cost."

Mike cut him short. "My mom can't read or write."

"Oh, okay, then just show her the bills and explain them!"

"That I will do!"

They both started to bag the groceries. Shylo looked up and asked, "Who filled out the information on that credit book?"

"I did."

He returned to bagging, but a moment later, stopped again. "Who signs her state checks?"

"I do."

Shylo looked at him for a moment and then grinned. It was really none of his business to begin with, and he didn't plan to carry it any further. They finished bagging the food, and he went to the front door and looked in both directions. Locking the front door, he returned and picked up a carton of Winston and one of the sacks.

They started to leave, carrying everything, and Shylo said, "Wow, over twenty-seven dollars! This is definitely our largest sale."

Twenty-five feet out the back, past the mostly missing, small picket fence and over the rolling, bare yard, they were at the front of Mike's house. Shylo looked up at the enormous trees casting a deep shade. He thought, *Funny how a few feet away the light is so dominating that it creates a different atmosphere.* With one step up, they climbed the wood porch that ran the width of the house. Two folding chairs and a wicker loveseat, with part of the wicker missing, dominated the porch. The good, organic mildew smell of living plants captured the attention, and a noticeable drop in temperature could be felt.

Mike yelled, "Open the door, Mom!"

The front door immediately opened, and they entered. Even with the front door open, the light in the room was like walking out of the sun into a dark movie theater. They stood there while their eyes dilated.

"Mr. Shylo, Mr. Shylo, please come in!"

He could now see the lady standing in front of him. She was almost four feet tall, obese, with a badly deformed right arm, wearing a one-piece dress and cloth slippers. The only difference on the inside was the furniture, and it was as worn out as the house. He looked back at the person in front of him. She had long, stringy hair, but a smile that welcomed you to her domain. The two boys took the sacks to the kitchen table.

She asked Shylo, "Can I get you a glass of lemonade?"

He could not help but feel that the friendly gesture was genuine, and he hated to turn her offer down. "No, ma'am, really, I have to get back to the store."

He handed her the carton of cigarettes. She opened it and threw Mike a pack. His eyebrows went up as he looked at Mike, and he admitted to himself that whenever Mike needs cigarettes for his mom, there would be no problem.

"I don't mean to be rude, but I really do have to get back. It was a pleasure meeting you." He stuck his right hand out and immediately said, "Oh!" He jerked the hand back and stuck out his left hand.

She grinned and shook his hand. "I'm Emily Toon."

"I'm Shylo Desmond, and I'll see you again."

"Goodbye, Mr. Shylo, and thank you."

CHAPTER FIVE

At 640 Jefferson Street, Shylo knocked sharply on the screen door. A large man with very short hair, wearing military pants, a white tank top and gray socks, answered.

"Yeah, what do you want?"

Shylo could hear Kathy in the background. "It's him, Nancy, it's him."

Quickly, Nancy was between her father and the door. "I got it, Daddy, it's for me!"

He backed off with a look of disgust. "The least you could do is introduce me!"

He left the room, and Nancy came out on the porch. She was dressed in white pants, white boat slippers and a light blue, double-breasted, long-sleeved blouse. It looked more like a riding outfit for horses than anything else. Shylo wore black Levi's, a black short-sleeved shirt with no undershirt and the top three buttons undone, a nice pair of brown loafers and black socks. She took him over to the porch swing to set down. He looked into the moist, vital richness of her big, beautiful eyes.

"You look very pretty today!"

"Thank you, you look very handsome, but I'm afraid the sun will eat you alive in that black outfit."

"There's not much sun in the evening."

"Then maybe I'll have to do the eating!"

He grinned real large at her in a funny way, but it was brought back down to a closed-lip grin when he saw how serious her grin was.

"Let me get us a glass of Kool-Aid." She got up and went in.

He was left looking in the window at her father. He was sitting on the couch with a newspaper positioned so that his head was pointed at the window. After a few minutes of uneasy fidgeting from being watched, she returned with two large glasses of Kool-Aid.

"Kathy is setting the game up next to the house. She wants to know if she can play too."

"Of course."

"We play knock away. Do you play it like that?"

"To tell you the truth, I've never played croquet; you'll have to teach me."

"No problem. It's kind of like baseball and golf, except you use wood mallets, wood balls and wire hoops. You put the hoops in the ground, spaced apart like baseball plates. Then you knock the ball through each hoop. If you hit another person's ball, you either get an extra turn or you can knock their ball away with yours."

"Sounds like fun. My mom wants to know if you would like to come over tomorrow for dinner? She's making her famous smothered chicken burritos. She makes the best hot sauce you ever ate. Even though she's from the East, she has always liked Mexican food."

Nancy sat for a moment and then lightly shook her head as she said, "Okay, what time?"

"On Sunday we generally eat between three p.m. and five p.m. We don't open the store."

"Sounds great. I'll be there. Shall we go see how Kathy's doing?"

"That would be good. I feel like a duck being eyed by the hunter."

She turned to look at the window and turned back. "I know. He won't hurt anyone."

"Does he dislike all boys?"

"No, just the ones who talk to his daughters."

CHAPTER SIX

It was almost three p.m. on Sunday, and Nancy prepared to knock on the screen door. She stopped—Shylo was already pushing the door open.

"Come in, everyone has been waiting to meet you."

She stepped from the small porch into his living room. "I'm not late, am I?"

"No, my family is just waiting to meet you." He turned to introduce her. Jim and Joyce sat on the couch, looking at her, while Cannon lay on the floor, watching TV. Shylo held out his hand to acknowledge his parents.

"This is my mom and dad, Joyce and Corey Desmond."

"It's Jim, Shylo, Jim." They both stood up to greet her.

Joyce remarked as she stood there shaking her hand, "You already met me, it just wasn't very formal."

They set back down, and he used the same hand gesture for his brother. "This is my brother, Cannon." He turned his head from the TV, grinned, held up his hand to wave and immediately turned back to the television.

He ushered her over to one of the two easy chairs to sit down in, then he sat in the other. She started to watch the television, but you could tell it was with a nervous attention.

Joyce finally broke the scene by asking, "How long have you lived here?"

"Fred, my father, was transferred to Beale AFB late last summer, and we rented our house around the corner instead of living at base housing. The worst thing about base housing on an Air Force base is the planes flying at all hours of the night. A place as close as Olivehurst can be just as bad if it's lined up with the runways, but Olivehurst isn't, and it's very seldom you hear a plane overhead."

Joyce was excited at her talking and asked, "Have you ever been stationed overseas?"

"Oh yes, we spent almost two years in Germany before we came here. My sister and I went to an American school there, but anytime you stepped off the base it was all Germany. The atmosphere, the language and the culture was so different there that I didn't speak to anyone off base."

Joyce made a face as she cocked her head. "Oh, that's too bad, honey. If you could have at least spoke German I bet you would have gotten along with them."

"I doubt it. Everything was so different there that I didn't like it. But it was probably no more different than it would be for a German in America."

"Well, I can understand that. It must be devastating to leave your home country and go to a totally different one for two years."

Jim and Shylo sat listening, dominated by the conversation of the two females. Finally, Jim spoke up, "How's dinner doing, honey?"

"Ah, I'm glad you said something." Joyce got up and went in the kitchen. A moment later she returned and announced, "A few more minutes and dinner will be ready." She looked at Nancy and grinned. "Maybe I could get you to help me set the table while I finish?"

Shylo spoke up. "Hey, I'm the one who invited her over!"

"Yeah, but I'm the one who asked you to invite her, so don't get your pants all in a knot."

Nancy grinned from ear to ear. It made her feel all warm inside to have anyone make such a fuss over her. He followed her into the kitchen to help set the table. The table was in an area that could be seen from the living room, but around the corner was the kitchen with everything in it. They set the table while Joyce brought out the food. Nancy admitted to everyone, "The only time I get to eat Mexican food is when we go out."

In just a few minutes the table held their meal. A large bread pan full of hot chicken burritos; two cut avocados; two bowls of chips; a bowl of sour cream; a bowl of hot, homemade smothering sauce; a bowl of shredded cheese; a small bowl of fresh hot peppers; and large glasses of sweet ice tea were at each plate.

With everyone seated at the table, Jim sat at the head and gave thanks to God. He also prayed that God would watch over his young men as they made their way in life. Joyce said amen a little bit louder than usual, and everyone started eating.

Nancy made mention of the tea first thing. "Wow, this stuff tastes great! How do you make tea that tastes like that?"

Joyce grinned and raised an eyebrow. "That's pre-sweetened Southern iced tea. The trick is to stir the sugar in the hot liquid and let it sit for five minutes covered before you finish filling the gallon container with ice or water."

"I'd like to have that recipe so I can make some. I never tasted iced tea that good."

After a few minutes she spoke again. "In fact, I'd like to have the recipe for the entire meal. My mom's a good cook, and I'm sure she'd like to know how to fix this meal."

Joyce spoke up again. "Well, next time you'll have to bring her with you, and we'll see if she likes it. In fact, you'll have to bring your father and sister too." Shylo winced at the idea of her father eyeballing him at his own table.

Nancy asked to be excused for the restroom, and Joyce took a long, hard look at the back of this voluptuous young lady as she walked away. Nancy wore a tight, dark Levi skirt that hung to the knees; a white short-sleeved blouse that left nothing to the imagination; and dark, smooth glossy patent leather shoes. When she walked, all the body parts moved in synchronized motion. For a moment, Joyce looked to play dumb, but then she looked straight at Jim's face and shook her head no.

Nancy returned, and Joyce reported with a large smile, "You don't know how we have been looking forward to your coming over. The only people we know are Jim's brother and family. Other than that, we have been looking forward to making friends with more people."

Cannon finished eating and returned to the front of the television. Jim followed him, and the girls started to clear the table. Shylo still sat at the table, wondering which way to go. Many times he had cleaned up everything by himself, but never with a female friend over. Of course, this was the first time he ever had one over. But still, his actions here would set the precedent for the future. He looked in the living room and then back at the kitchen. Suddenly he just stood up and started to clear the table. He avoided his mother's grin and Nancy's look, with her mouth open, and continued to help as if it could be no other way.

When everything was done, Joyce brought out the family picture album and invited Nancy to sit back at the table with her. Shylo's body already felt numb from the embarrassment he had taken so far, but he knew every picture and every incriminating, bone tickling story that lay ahead. Just before setting down, he spoke to his father, whose complete attention was directed at the TV set. "If I fall down on the floor, will you come pound on my chest to get it going again?"

Jim grinned but never took his eyes off the television. Joyce looked at her son as if she had just noticed his presence.

"Do you feel okay, honey? Maybe you should just go lay down for a while. Nancy and I have everything under control." She turned and opened the album to the first page while Nancy watched and listened with much eagerness. He didn't look at the pictures, it wasn't necessary, but he listened to each story and wondered how she could remember every word so accurately. They started with him, a very small, naked baby, lying on his back, with a large grin, and urinating straight up in the air like a little fountain. The final story was from a picture of her holding a fishing pole and frowning, and how she would have caught that old cat fish if the boys would have left her alone. The final page always brought the same conclusion. "I've got more pictures, and I need to do another book, but I just never seem to have the time."

Shylo thought, *Yeah, right, like the first one isn't humiliating enough.*

CHAPTER SEVEN

On the Fourth of July, Shylo stood in front of Jim as he came in to give him a lunch break. "We have a problem in the meat department!"

"What is it?"

"For the third time since we opened, I've been chewed out by a customer over the hamburger."

"What was the problem?"

"Well, Uncle Harry says that when you add more or new meat to the tray, you pack it around the old meat. Three times I've had people come back and complain about getting that brown meat that they couldn't see until they got home and opened the package. This old boy today, well, I won't tell you what he had to say, but it was rather vulgar."

He put his hand on Shylo's shoulder and addressed the problem. "We haven't been open for that long, so for the time being let's do it Harry's way."

Shylo's head dropped as he stood in front of his father. "Well, after he left, Aunt Martha came in and got some stuff. When I offered her their book to write it down, she gave me a dirty look and just kept marching out the door."

"Okay, I'll have to talk with Uncle Harry and we'll find out what he wants to do. Just remember that everything's OK and keep doing what you're doing, all right?"

He looked up and grinned, "Okay, Dad."

"Now go get something to eat so I can go to work, and I'll see if I can bring some fireworks home tonight."

Mechanically, the days of July stepped back into history, just as they had been occupied; no more, no less. The same problems always seemed to be different, but the days of life hold the reproof for his instructions, and the wise will give thanks for the privilege of being there for the challenge.

The first of August dropped in and reinforced the summer heat, with a high of over ninety degrees every day. The everyday temperature affected everyone's attitude. It seemed to bring out the worst in even the best of people.

One day at about one p.m., when the sun had peaked and was falling, and the temperature had risen to ninety-six and was holding fast, Shylo was standing behind the counter, talking to Nancy. The noise of sirens could be heard in the distance and continued to get louder. They stepped out the front door to look and see.

A motorcycle was coming off the cloverleaf at a break-neck speed. The bike slid on its side, tearing down the Stop sign and throwing its driver across the main street into an empty ditch. Nancy screamed at the idea of watching someone get killed. Six police cars converged upon the scene. A few minutes later an ambulance arrived. They loaded the rider on a stretcher and put him in the vehicle. An officer followed them with his gun drawn. They made him get back out. Finally he holstered the gun and was allowed to get in. The ambulance left, and Shylo and Nancy went back inside.

A few minutes later a patrol car pulled in front of the store, and a young officer got out and went in. Nancy met him at the door. "Did that guy get killed?"

"No, the world couldn't be that lucky." He walked over to the pop machine and retrieved a bottle of Coke. She followed and asked what happened.

"Oh, just a high-speed chase." He had the comical personality of an overactive officer. "Mr. Evel Knievel, and I put the emphasis on 'evil,' knocked over the First National Bank in Lynda, two miles to the north. We almost stopped him there, but he deliberately shot a bystander, and we had to back off. Then he jumped on that racing motorcycle that was hidden next to the building and was gone. That bike is history now, but we're afraid that since he exited in Olivehurst, he probably lives here. We have a hundred little places like this to cover, but it seems like we're always in Olivehurst. If there's anything big going down, you always end up in Olivehurst. Do you guys know him or anything about what happened?"

"No, sir."

106

He took a business card out of his shirt pocket and handed it to Shylo. Sitting the now-empty bottle on the counter, he said, "Well, if you do hear anything, please give us a call." He turned to leave but came back grinning.

"How much for the Coke?"

"Ten cents."

He handed Shylo a dime and left.

Shylo looked at Nancy. "If the Marysville police are always in Olivehurst, where are they? I never see them. I don't look for them, but still I never see them. And their cars are a little hard to miss."

She shrugged her shoulders and remarked, "Maybe they're always under cover."

"Under cover for what? To catch the old lady across the street jaywalking." She looked at him with a very deep "I couldn't care less" look.

CHAPTER EIGHT

Systematically, one day at a time, the uneventful middle of August arrived. Shylo, who had since been the proud recipient of a California driver's license, was being hailed to the front door on a Sunday morning. Usually his mom and dad were still asleep, but they were the ones doing the hailing. Unaware of what the problem was, he wandered to the front door to see.

Looking out on the front lawn, his heart stopped beating and his mind went blank, but his eyes still worked. A 1957 red and white two-door Ford Fairlane convertible with a black top was parked crossways on the front lawn. He made a fist and beat on his own chest to get it working again. Jim and Joyce stood next to the vehicle, grinning and pointing at it. Coughing, he stepped outside to see it better. Without a scratch anywhere, the paint job shined intensely. The top was still in the state of looking brand-new. The black and white factory-designed seats looked untouched. The black dashboard and steering column still shined from being recently cleaned, and the black vinyl floorboard seemed to be spotless. The power plant was a standard 312 V8 with a manual three-speed transmission. Everything worked and was still original, except for two things. The column stick for changing gears had been taken off, and a conversion floor-mounted shifter had been installed. This gave the car a sportier look and feel. The two factory taillight lenses had been replaced with flat ones. This gave the round part under the fins a barrel-like affect, and a customized look that was very appealing. Jim watched as his son finished his inspection.

"If it was mine, I'd put the top down and go for a ride, but it's yours, not mine. Your keys are already in the ignition."

Jim and Joyce walked into the house, leaving Shylo, who still hadn't spoken a word. He walked around the car again, touching the metal like a child in a fantasy land. Then he opened the driver's door and got in. He touched the seat to make sure it was real. The feel sent a message back to his brain that it really was there. Starting the motor and adjusting the radio, he backed onto the driveway and pulled out on the street. A new song was playing on the AM station from Yuba City, and he listened to it for the first time. It was "Daydream Believer" by the Monkees.

By the time realization had set in he had picked Nancy up and was motoring down the freeway to nowhere in mind. After two hours of riding with the top down, she was simply exhausted. He took her home and went back to his house to just sit in a lawn chair and look at his vehicle.

CHAPTER NINE

The inevitable days of school prevailed, and Joyce traded work schedules with Shylo since school didn't get out until after three p.m. He didn't relieve her until four p.m. He took a few minutes to drive home, a moment to drop Nancy off, a few minutes to change clothes, eat or do whatever, and then went to the store. Anyone could see the store was going in the opposite direction of what was planned. There was never money left over to put into the business. When the bank payment, utilities and vendors were totaled, it always outweighed what went into the till.

The winter was almost over before the Desmond brothers sat down and discussed the problem of the store and how to solve it. For the first time in weeks, Uncle Harry showed up on Saturday with a smile. Five weeks later he left. He was transferred to Ft. Campbell, Tennessee.

The store was now closed on Saturday and Sunday. At the beginning of winter they had started closing at six p.m. and decided to leave it like that. Because of the strong military rules, Harry's name was not on anything to begin with. So he could leave and not be connected. Then at the end of May, when school was over, Jim's family would abandon the store and move back East.

One week of school left, and Jim called everyone to a meeting at the kitchen table. With everyone at the table, looking at him, he started talking.

"Okay, I won't beat around the bush, we'll get straight to business. Friday, I talked to Mr. Joseph Johnson, the regional manager for Red Horse Van Lines, and he made me a very interesting proposition. A freight company in

Salt Lake City, Utah, known as Beehive Transfer, needs a household goods warehouse opened and established as soon as possible. Beehive is a very successful business, even since the days of horse and buggy. They have long since accumulated the intrastate moving rights for Utah, and the interstate moving rights for seven Western states. These rights have never been utilized, and recently they were informed by the Department of Transportation that if the rights were not put to use immediately, they would be pulled. If you look at the stenciling on the passenger door of an over-the-road commercial truck, you'll see an motor carrier number. This is generally a seven-digit figure. But if it was a Beehive vehicle it would only be four digits, and the first two of those would be zeros. This small number tells you how long ago it was issued. Red Horse is interested in buying the interstate rights in the future. But for right now the only way to protect those rights is for Beehive to open a moving company in Salt Lake City, Utah. According to the influential Mr. J.J., if I would be willing to engage and participate in this activity for Beehive, then Red Horse would be interested in a man of my capability when the transaction took place. We only need to pack and be ready to move when school is out."

Shylo asked, "What about the store?"

"You're not to tell anyone what we are doing. We'll continue doing everything as normal until we leave, and after that it just won't open anymore. The sign will say closed and the door will be locked."

Their furniture was scheduled to be moved eight days after school was out. The truth about what was going on proved to be impossible to keep from Nancy. She summarized to Shylo, "You don't just pack everything in boxes and then leave them there for storage."

Jim quit his job before school was out and went to Salt Lake to meet his new boss and find a place to rent. He would be back before the move.

At first Nancy was not affected by the news, but the closer moving day got, the more she wanted to be with Shylo. He didn't feel the same way, but he would never admit this to Nancy.

The day finally arrived when their furniture was being loaded, and Shylo had the store open for the last time. Jim had returned and everything was now a go for the Salt Lake project. Shylo told Mike that day that their credit book had been destroyed, and he would leave the back door unlocked that night. There wasn't a lot left in the store, but he and his mother was welcome to whatever they wanted.

At six p.m. he took Nancy home for the last time. He stood in front of both her parents, in their front yard, saying goodbye. After the second time she reminded him to write, her mother spoke up.

"He already said he was going to write, now what else can he do?" Her father stood there watching, without saying a word. He acted like a prayer had been answered, and he was patiently waiting the conclusion.

For a moment Shylo thought, *The older his girls get, the more that old man will suffer*. Then he grinned for a moment, said goodbye and left.

The Desmond family slept on blankets that night in an empty house. At four a.m. they left for Salt Lake City. Jim and Joyce rode in the Pontiac Tempest station wagon, and Shylo and Cannon in the Ford Fairlane convertible. Jim had rented a house and wanted to make sure they were there to except their furniture.

1967
Salt Lake City

chapter one

In the middle of June 1964, Jim rented an L-shaped warehouse in Salt Lake City, Utah. For the next two days he walked around the building with a clipboard, making a list of what he would need to operate a functioning household goods warehouse. Shylo, who was seventeen years old now, assisted his father without question to help him get started. The Beehive Transfer office was on the west edge of the city, behind the Union Pacific building. The company was successfully run by two brothers whose characteristics of old age exhibited a loss of mental faculties associated with the end of a physiological cycle of erosion. The brothers were named Jim and John Holstead; Jim wore a suit to the office and was in charge of the eight-person staff. John wore a sports coat and was in charge of the twenty-nine drivers and workers, two mechanics and a three-man bull gang who specialized in moving heavy objects. One of their two railroad docks, the main one, lay just north of the Union Pacific building. Train cars were unloaded on the west side, and the trucks were loaded on the east side. The goods, everything from new shoes to sixteen hundred pound rolls of paper, were delivered out appropriately. About a hundred and fifty feet existed between the west side and the east side of this dock. In the center was a large type warehouse with an endless sequence of overhanging doors on both sides. The cement floor was the height of a box car and did not take much of a metal plate to make a walk-board. When a box car was unloaded, the contents were generally wheeled straight across the dock to the appropriate truck. If there was no truck, then the goods would be stacked up on the dock.

This dock was over a city block long, divided off and inhabited by various freight companies. Beehive's section was somewhere in the middle, two hundred and fifty feet long. Inside on the south wall was an after-the-fact wood shed that served as the foreman's office, with a large window overlooking the dock. This crude shack that looked like it belonged in a tree was where all the Beehive workers reported in the morning, unless they had other instructions. Even with the building being made of metal, if you walked around the entire structure you would swear there was enough cement there to have built another Hoover Dam.

Many years ago when John had trouble with an unruly driver, he hired the biggest, toughest, ugliest-looking man he could find to be the dock foreman, Mr. Armstrong Woosley. With reference to reputation, his nickname was, to say the least, "Arm." All the men reported to him, and if Arm said you were fired, then there was no reason to question his authority. John was not trying to create a mean company, but a company that could deal with mean people. Otherwise, John spent his time fulfilling his position by driving around in his new Lincoln Continental. And you better be working or observing your lunch hour when he went by. Otherwise, the Arm would cast you into the ranks of the unemployed.

The other dock was less than half the size of the Union Pacific one, with no office of any kind, and was used more or less for backup during heavy workdays. This dock was in the Rio Grande building, south of Second South at about Nine Hundred West.

Friday afternoons in the summertime, there was always a show at this corner. In front of the bar called Happy Hour, next to the railroad tracks, would be something too hot to handle. Generally wearing more makeup than clothing, always credited as a professional to her profession. The same girl was never there more than a few minutes before being picked up and immediately, if not sooner, a new one was there to take her place. Excluding the spiked heels, she would be wearing less clothes and more makeup than the preceding girl. The police department, because of complaining citizens, was always trying to clean the street up but wasn't very successful. They would arrest a number of girls, give them a ticket for soliciting sex and then put them in jail. By the next day the girls would all be out, with their forty-five dollar ticket paid, and back on the same corner doing business. Their name and crime would be listed in the newspaper. This was considered advertisement, and nothing was thought about it. Then one day the law was changed. Entrapment was redefined, and the procedure was changed. A female officer dressed like a prostitute and referred to as a meter maid would issue a ticket to the man for soliciting sex, and then arrest him. His name and offense would go in the newspaper, and this was breaking up a lot of good marriages and happy family lives. This cleaned up the famous Second South and moved the girls to the truck stop and other sources.

CHAPTER TWO

A large dirt lot behind the Beehive offices contained the company's equipment. An all-metal, unpainted mechanic shop was on the north side of the offices, with a diesel fuel pump behind the shop. Visible after entering the lot was two longtime standing, antiquated stacks of horse-drawn wagons. If you come through here looking for Beehive's name painted all over the side of something, you were out of luck. The small, one-level office building had their name printed legibly on a small sign over the front door. Their trucks and trailers had an even smaller sign on each side that was easily put on or removed by hand. Other than that, the only place you could find their name was in the phone book or on their paperwork. At a time when other companies were looking at the free advertising space on their own equipment, these people still considered the cost was a bigger negative than the advertising was a plus. It was hard to realize how they had incorporated such a financially strong firm, but the truth is they had inherited it, along with the hundred-year-old rules and policies they operated by.

CHAPTER THREE

That evening at the dinner table in the Desmond home, Jim said, "I was at the main office all afternoon with our accountant, Mr. Johnny Gay. You should have been there. Two weeks ago Beehive received three new forty-nine thousand dollar Kenworths. The local bank had two men there in black suits all afternoon, trying to convince Jim and John to finance the trucks through their bank. Not that Beehive buys new trucks all the time, but they had to get these or lose their largest government account. Mr. Gay spent all afternoon telling them that the company policy was 'We buy a truck, drive it for thirty days, then write out a check to pay it off. I bet I heard him say that a hundred times. Tomorrow I'm going to order everything I need to open a warehouse."

"Honey, what is their largest account?"

"Believe it or not, the transportation of missiles."

"What kind of missiles?"

"The dangerous kind that can kill everyone."

Joyce looked across the table with a straight, sober face.

Cannon spoke up next. "Why do we need something that dangerous?"

Shylo answered, "To protect everyone."

Cannon looked Shylo straight in the face and answered with one long word. "RRRRRRRRRight!"

"You know I worry about you, little brother. Your idea of taking care of something is to have somebody else do it!"

Cannon paused before coming back with, "I've noticed that about you; you worry too much."

Joyce jumped in, "Okay, boys. All right, that's enough!"

Suddenly everyone turned their heads to what was on the television visible from the table: mass hysteria in the New York ship harbor. Thousands of girls were screaming from the climax of what was too much. Four young men coming down a gang plank singing, 'I Want to Hold Your Hand.' The young men were original in sound and looks. Their hair came down halfway over the ears and was combed straight down without being trained to lay in any other direction. They were dressed all in black with black ties and white shirts. Their group name was The Beatles. They were not actually singing the song live; that came from a hidden source as they strutted down the movable bridge. All four of the young men were wearing a smile of pure delight at their being welcomed to a country by so many beautiful young virgins screaming with lust. This arrival was on February 7, 1964, four months ago, but was still being played on various TV programs.

1973
A NEW MENU

cHapter one

Six years later, Shylo sat in the waiting room of the small local business, Jason's Trucking, on Redwood Road in Salt Lake City. He rested his head on the back of the chair, thinking back to five years before, when Jim and Joyce moved to Louisville, Kentucky, after Jim accepted a position with Red Horse Van Lines. Jim's new job was as regional manager for the Great Lakes area. A regional manager sets up a local intrastate carrier to represent the larger interstate carrier. This job was why Jim had been instrumental in opening a warehouse for Beehive Transfer in Salt Lake City. After Red Horse Van Lines purchased Beehive's seven interstate rights in the West, they were true to their word about being interested in Jim. The local rights and moving company were sold lock, stock and barrel to another interested party.

This brought thoughts of his younger brother Cannon, who had joined the Army Air Corp. He said he would be better off to enlist than to be drafted into the Vietnam conflict.

On his first leave, he announced with much bitterness and confusion, "When we got to boot camp they unloaded the bus and lined the enlisted men up on one side and the drafted men on the other. They apologized to the drafted men, said they knew they didn't want to be there, and they would make their stay as pleasant as possible. Then they turned around and looked at the enlisted men with a certain air of hostility. They started yelling and never quit. Nothing is ever said in a normal tone; it's always a blood-chilling scream, and anything you say better be with the same kind if yell."

After a period of time it became clear to Cannon what was going on. The word draftee meant that you didn't want to be there in the first place, but because of circumstances, there you were. But when your time was served you could leave. The word enlisted meant that you had personally chosen this and were interested in making it your career. Therefore, you would be given every opportunity available for advancement in rank, education or anything the government had to offer. But first you had to be a soldier, and the first thing any soldier learns is to fight. Without learning this you would not qualify to be in the United States Armed Forces.

During his tour in Vietnam he started out learning to work on helicopters by cleaning parts for the mechanics. He learned how to fly one by riding with the chopper pilots who flew missions. After taking a number of required courses, he became a qualified pilot for the Hundred and First Airborne Division in the Army Air Corp.

Two years ago he married Sheila Jenkins, a girl he had been dating since high school in Salt Lake City, and was now stationed in Fort Campbell, Kentucky. This was the same little brother who expressed a strong disapproval for such power weapons that were used for protection.

Shylo never enlisted, nor was drafted. He never knew why he wasn't drafted when most others were being called up. When he turned eighteen he registered for the draft at the post office but was never contacted.

During his final year of high school he met the girl of his dreams, Mary Allbright. They were both in their senior year of high school, and after three months of knowing her, he told Cannon that she was the girl he was going to marry. But then, halfway through the school year, something awful happened. Shylo wrecked his car— the beautiful '57 Fairlane convertible— o his way home from school one day. He had no idea what happened, just that while coming to a stop, the brake pedal went all the way to the floor. Before he knew what had taken place, a telephone pole had caved in the front end. He was the only person in the car and in the accident. If it hadn't been for the steering wheel, he would have been thrown out through the windshield. Anyway, looking at it in the school parking lot was the last time he ever saw his car. The vehicle and the pole were totaled out. He had been knocked out by the steering wheel, transported to the hospital by ambulance, admitted and released on the same day.

A couple weeks later Jim helped him get another vehicle for transportation, a 1947 Packard automatic with a straight eight. It was dull gray and missing the left front fender. Shylo replaced it with one from the junkyard, a shiny black one, and he left it that way. He finished his last year of school and went to work full time at the warehouse. He was the only person working for Beehive under the age of twenty-one. Then, at the age of nineteen, Shylo and Mary ran away to get married. They told no one of their plans and rented a furnished apartment. With amazement at how easy it was, they secretly moved their clothes and personal belongings to the apartment. The closest they came to getting caught was at ten p.m. when Cannon walked up the driveway on his way home after watching a movie with a friend. Shylo had just finished putting the rest of his clothes in the car when he spotted Cannon in the darkness. Afraid that they had been discovered, he joined Mary, who was standing at the front of the car. Cannon looked in the car on his way by and then stopped in front of Shylo and Mary.

He grinned real big and asked, "What are you two gonna do, run away and get married?"

Without waiting for an answer, Cannon went into the house, not having the slightest idea that he had just hit the nail on the head.

Late on a hot July night, they notified their parents by leaving notes and ran away to Las Vegas to get married. Immediately after their marriage, the fights for dominant power were a constant battle. The boy of her dreams and the girl of his desire took on different roles when the decisions of life were not subject to parental control.

Then, after two years, they had a baby boy, Dustin James Desmond. Dustin was the buffer that held them together, but the daily part of association between Mary and Shylo became a chore and not a pleasure. After Mary had Dustin they moved into a two-bedroom duplex with a garage. Shylo set up a wood shop in the garage and started building tables for a hobby.

After four years of marriage they split up and divorced. He moved into a one-room apartment downtown, and she retained the duplex. For two months she had been working as a customer service representative for First West Airlines, and was doing great. Of course, Jim and Joyce wanted Shylo to come back home and move to Kentucky, but they didn't press the issue when he refused.

After the warehouse was sold and his parents moved away, he was twenty-two years old and working at the dock with a chauffeur's license. After months on end of unloading boxcars under the watchful eye of Arm, it started to get to his ego. The dreary days of delivering out freight in the little straight-bed trucks, whose density looked as much rust as metal, got to be too much.

He was twenty-three years old now and a qualified, licensed driver, but the jobs that involved the bigger, nicer equipment went to the older drivers. In the early spring of 1973 he applied for a driving position with Jason's Trucking, a produce hauler that required three trips a week to California and back. Having a legal Utah chauffeur's license, he was hired on the spot after a quick driving test by the company's dispatcher. The guy had a lot of experience at hauling produce, and it showed. His name was Red Jameson, and for over an hour he fed Shylo with necessary information about the business. Shylo admitted this was a new menu, and he had a lot to learn.

Red's reply was, "With what you already know this won't take long to pick up."

Shylo was assigned an older cab-over Freightliner with a one-quarter sleeper, a six-cylinder Cummins and a ten-speed Road Ranger. This was the truck that all their new drivers started out in, and if he would have left they would have dispatched him out that very day. But he wanted to give at least one day's notice to Beehive.

Much to his dismay, and to everybody else at Beehive, Mr. Armstrong never showed up at his meager office the next morning. After forty-five minutes of eighteen men waiting to be dispatched, John showed up and took over. All he would say about Arm was that he was in the hospital in critical condition, and that was all he knew. Later, everyone found out that the preceding evening Arm was on Seventh East, stopped at a red light on his way home from the store. Next to him was a carload of teenagers, not one over nineteen years old. One of the teens said something derogatory to him. Of course, he returned the remark with an even lower opinion. When the light turned green he drove away, not knowing the danger he was in. They followed him to his house, and on his small front porch they bludgeoned him until his body was left for dead. He lay in a fetal position on the porch among the groceries he had been carrying. He was divorced and lived by himself, but a neighbor who was watching got a description of the boys, their vehicle and the license plate number. He called the police and reported the incident. Arm survived, but didn't have the ability to remember his own name after that.

CHAPTER TWO

Red came out from a room behind the counter in Jason's office. Holding a clipboard, he looked at Shylo.

"Are you hooked up and ready to roll?"

"Yes, sir, for about the last hour."

"Well, let's go get a hub reading, and you can be on your merry little way."

He grinned at this statement and led Shylo out the side door. Next to the building they walked up to the wheels of a silver forty-foot refer trailer. Red bent over to the outside of the wheels on the front axle and recorded the mileage off the hub meter. He handed Shylo a large brown envelope that contained his paperwork. On the back of this envelope was a place to write the mileage. He bent down on one knee, copied the numbers, then stood up and verified them with Red.

The dispatcher asked, "Did you fill the Thermo-King tank?"

"Yes, the tank is full."

The trailer, or refer unit, was a large refrigerator controlled by the Thermo-King unit mounted on the front of the trailer. It would keep the temperature inside at whatever the thermostat was set for. Three large pin lights were visible in the driver's side mirror. The lights were red, yellow and green, and the thermostat was next to these lights. Green meant the temperature inside was the same as the thermostat setting. Yellow meant the temperature wasn't the same, but the unit was running to correct this. Red meant the temperature wasn't the same and the unit wasn't running, and if your load depended upon this scale of degrees to stay fresh or frozen, you better get it fixed now.

The Thermo-King ran off diesel fuel supplied from a small tank in the center underneath the trailer. Forgetting to fuel this tank or having no knowledge of how much was in it was an unforgivable mistake.

On this trip the trailer was loaded with skids of cheese for San Francisco, California. The return load would involve a drive north on 101 to three different locations for a mixed load of vegetables. Shylo's pay was fourteen cents a mile, and the days were long and hard.

It was late July, and he had only been pulling for Jason's since the middle of May, but he was still waiting for what he considered a good trip. Red said goodbye and returned to the office. He climbed up in the cab, started the motor and filled out his logbook. While writing in the book, he made a mental check of his activities. The oil had been checked, all fuel tanks were full, the tires had been bumped, the trailer brakes were adjusted, the thermo unit was running and set at thirty-eight degrees, and his tool box was in the jock box on the passenger's side. *Yes,* he thought, *this one is going to be that good trip. The one where nothing goes wrong. I'll deliver the cheese tomorrow, load the vegetables and be back on the fourth day in time for the yard man to deliver it out.*

He put the ten-speed in second, released the brakes and pulled out of the yard with a renewed confidence for the trip. Then the reality of what a good trip would be set in. He would get paid for about fifteen hundred miles. At fourteen cents a mile, that would only be two hundred and ten dollars for four days work; that wasn't enough money. The yard man took care of loading and unloading trailers at home, but the driver was still responsible for loading and unloading out of town. Even though this was generally done by forklift, you still had to assist or wait until it was done. A few minutes later he turned west on Interstate 80. With the Wasatch Range in his rear view mirror, he leveled out for California.

The next day his drop in San Francisco went well, and he managed to get two of his three pick-ups that afternoon. The next morning he loaded the third one and then pointed his unit south for the trip home. He was in the mountains and unfamiliar territory on 101. As expected, he was grossing out at over eighty-one thousand pounds, and his paperwork contained the necessary overweight permits. At a very slow pace, he topped a six percent grade with the transmission in its third hole. As he started down the other side, he realized that third was too low. Knowing that he shouldn't have done it in the first place, but forgetting, he tried to change gears after starting down. The rule of thumb is to use the same gear going down that you used to go up. If you use a higher gear going down, change it on top of the hill. If you try to change it going down, once the gearshift is in neutral it won't go back in any gear as long as the weight of the vehicle is pushing it downhill. Still, this shouldn't be a problem. All you do is come to a stop, put the truck in gear and go on. The trouble was that it wouldn't stop. Pressing hard on the brake pedal and holding the handle for the trailer down would slow the unit up, but it was still progressively gaining speed. Shortly, the air pressure was too low to be effective, and the eight trailer wheels were bellowing out black smoke. The tractor was now shaking so hard from the speed that he was using the steering wheel to hold on to. The speedometer was maxed out and the vehicle was doing over a hundred miles an hour. The freeway was two lanes going down and three going up, with a very small pull over lane.

He looked at the terrain and thought, *The first one of those curves I come to, it will all be over with.* With his flashers going, his headlights flashing and pulling on the air horn intermittently, he was passing everyone on the left. Then down the road an orange and white VW van pulled into the left lane to go around someone. The sight took Shylo's breath. With a matter of seconds to make up his mind, he decided what to do. There was not enough room to go around on either side. The front wheel would go off the pavement, and at forty miles an hour with power steering you would lose control, let alone at over a hundred miles an hour with no power steering. He lined the truck up with the back of the VW and prayed for God to forgive him. Just before hitting it, the van pulled back in the right lane. Shylo caught a glimpse of it in the mirror after he went by. It was rocking so hard that the driver almost lost control. You could see the bottom of the hill was going to level out without that curve that would cause the truck to run amuck.

Breathing hard, Shylo yelled, "I'm gonna live! I'm gonna live!"

He rolled to a stop on the side of the road and sat there, holding on to the steering wheel for fifteen minutes. He never felt more alive in his life and was grinning from ear to ear.

Later he realized that he never saw the VW when it went by or who was in it. Slowly he realized what had happened and why the truck wouldn't stop. He pushed in on the parking valve for the trailer and tried to pull forward. The vehicle wouldn't move. He released this valve, pushed in on the parking valve for the tractor and tried to pull forward. The unit moved forward with nothing stopping it. He felt like an idiot. He had been hooking up units for a long time, and you always test both brakes. You want the trailer brakes slightly tighter to prevent jack-knifing. When you are full and coming down a steep hill, it takes both sets of brakes to stop. He could remember Red being so fanatical about adjusting the trailer brakes.

When Shylo had asked him about the tractor brakes, he replied, "Don't ever adjust the brakes on the drivers; our mechanics will take care of those."

Finally, he got out and adjusted the brakes on the drive axles. Then he pulled the parking valve out for the tractor and tried to pull forward. The vehicle still wouldn't move. Again, he got out and made a long, slow visual inspection of both the trailer and the tractor. It looked like everything had remained intact, and the light was shining green on the Thermo unit. With no apparent damage and nothing better to do, he got back in, turned off the flashers and slowly pulled back out on the highway. Later, he wouldn't say anything about what had happened, but the valuable lesson he learned would not be forgotten.

Like he figured, he pulled back into the yard on the fourth day. Before he could get out of the cab, Red came out to take the mileage off the trailer. He met him at the trailer wheels.

Red asked, "Where have you been? You should have been back here yesterday."

While writing the mileage down on the back of his trip envelope, he answered him, "I guess I should have run harder. Maybe if I took something to keep me awake at night."

He totaled his mileage and looked at Red. "Sixteen hundred and eighty miles."

For a moment the two looked at each other. Then Red turned and went inside. Shylo followed to turn his envelope into the accountant. He expected any moment to be fired by the owner or Red.

To his dismay, he was set up to go to L.A. the next day. To top everything off, Red asked him to take a trailer to be loaded with grain, and this would be his load for the Pillsbury plant in L.A. It only took about eighteen minutes to load it, and it would really help out because the yard man was swamped with work.

The next morning, Shylo loaded a sheet of plywood and some brown butcher paper on a forty foot refer trailer. He hooked his tractor up to it and drove to the farm co-op silos next to Ogden. After obtaining a tare weight on the platform truck scale, he backed the unit up to a designated loading area behind the extremely gigantic cement block cylinders. He latched open one of the back doors and left the other door locked shut. A man with a twelve-inch-wide hose attached to an underground tube system got up in the trailer and, pulling back on a handle at the end of the hose, he started to blow grain up in the front. Shylo folded the butcher paper over one side of the plywood and put it on its side in the doorway with the paper facing in the trailer. The man with the hose finished loading the grain a little less than four feet high throughout the trailer.

Shylo closed the door and pulled around the side to get a gross weight and an axle weight. With the two thousand overweight permit per tandem, he was allowed to weigh thirty-four thousand pounds on the drive axles and trailer axles. The weight came to within five hundred pounds of each. He thought, *It's amazing how that guy knows how much grain to blow in. I wonder what his trick is.*

He drove back to the yard to make ready to go. This time, Red and Shylo recorded the mileage before Shylo went to load it. With a sound of certainty, he informed Red, "If I so much as have a flat tire on this trip, I'll quit when I get back!"

Red listened but never said a word. Shylo remembered what he had been told yesterday.

Red returned, "It only takes eighteen minutes for them to load the grain."

"They were right, eighteen minutes for that guy to blow it on, but it was three hours ago I left here to go get it. A total of about forty miles at fourteen cents a mile is only seven dollars and twenty cents. I hope the yard man gets paid by the hour and not mileage."

He finished getting the vehicle ready while the office did his paperwork. This time he adjusted the tractor brakes as well as the trailer. On the tractor, you tighten the adjusting linkage down tight and then back it off three quarter turns. The trailer is the same process, except you only back the linkage off one quarter turn.

His paperwork was completed, his logbook filled out, and again he left for California. This trip, he was headed through Las Vegas for the L.A. area. He would deliver the grain to the Pillsbury plant, where he had been before, and pick up a return load of cabbage just south of L.A.

As he rounded Point of the Mountain, he looked in the mirror for a last glimpse of the Salt Lake Valley. He could see rubber flying in the air behind him. With the tractor and trailer pulling so smooth, it took a moment for him to realize that he was peeling a tire.

He pulled over and got out. The left front outside tire on the trailer was totally destroyed. The inside tire was going flat while he stood there. He could hear the hissing of the escaping air. That side of the axle was slowly dropping to the ground. For a moment, he stood there looking and thought, *Well, I'm sure glad I looked in the mirror before those rims hit the pavement.* He set out his reflectors, dropped the trailer and drove to the nearest phone to call the office. He worried that maybe they would let him go on the spot.

Red sent out two tires and a service truck. With the rubber replaced, he continued on. The cab smelled like diesel, but the inside of that cab always smelled like diesel.

For a few hours, everything went well. Then, twenty miles away from Las Vegas, the motor quit running. It would turn over and try to start, but it wouldn't start. It acted like it was out of fuel, but the fuel filter was full. Twice in the past he had replaced the pump and that cured the problem. Both times the pump came from the International shop in Vegas. Two weeks earlier he put the second pump on while sitting in the dirt lot between the International shop and the King's Eight Casino. While he was doing this, Las Vegas was having a windy day. He opened the passenger door to get to the toolbox that was on the floorboard. At that moment a microburst of wind blew into the cab, sucked his trip envelope out of the sleeper, and blew it over the top of all three levels of the King's Eight Motel. He searched but never found it. Before talking to his office, he thought, *Even I wouldn't believe this story.* But the only thing absolutely necessary in that envelope was the bill of lading and weight tickets, and the office could mail copies out.

He tried to start the truck again, with no luck. It was now after midnight, and he decided to wait until morning and try it again. If it still wouldn't start, he would hitch a ride to a phone and find out what they wanted to do with their truck.

The next morning was the same thing; you could spray starting fluid into the breather and it would try to start until the vapor was quickly gone, and then it would just turn over. He locked up the cab and hitched a ride with another trucker into town. After explaining everything to Red on the phone, Red said to have the unit towed to the International shop and find out what it was going to take to get a fuel pump that worked. A hundred and twenty dollars later for the tow, the unit was in the lot.

With a feeling of despair, he went into the parts place and was waited on by an older gentleman who seemed to be waiting for him. As he explained the problem he couldn't help but think, *I bet Red's already talked to this guy.*

When he finished, the gentleman looked at him and grinned. "I find it hard to believe that those fuel pumps are that defective!" He went behind the counter, picked a brass fuel line fitting out of a box, turned and said, "Let's go take a look at it."

When he was showed the pump, he followed the fuel line to an inline fitting between the pump and the tanks. He pointed out a hairline fracture in the fitting and how the chassis underneath was stained with diesel fuel. Then he explained, "This is the inlet side of the pump. When the temperature has been getting high enough or whatever other factor, the pump has been sucking air through that crack. If it had been on the other side of the pump, it would have squirted diesel like a spray can." He held up the fitting he had in his hand. It was the same one that was cracked. "Put this on there, and it will take care of the problem."

He handed him the new fitting and walked away. A few minutes later it was on and the vehicle started like a brand new truck. He grinned and then thought, *I don't know what I'm excited about; this is going to be my last trip with this company. First of all, I'll report in, have something to eat and, in the words of a famous man, I'll 'make another mile.'*

Early the next morning he made the delivery to the Pillsbury plant; this one always amazed him, and he enjoyed watching the procedure. On a designated platform, you came to a stop, left the motor running and released the brakes. A person came out and chalked all the wheels. After this you got out of the truck and opened the back doors. You latched both doors open with the appropriate levers, retrieved the plywood and butcher paper that would fall out under a certain amount of grain, and then moved out of the way. The platform was level with the ground with only a one-inch gap around its sides. The front of this horizontal flat surface would slowly lift in the air, and forty thousand pounds of grain would slide out the back. It would lift to a point that you would swear the vehicle was going to fall too, but it never did. The grain went through a trapdoor into a chamber below the surface, and the front of the platform would slowly come back down. A few blocks away was a spray wash. You threw the butcher paper away and rinsed out the inside of the trailer.

A few miles away he spotted the trailer at the door of a large produce warehouse, and by noon he was loaded and ready to return home. Before he got to the truck stop to fuel up for the return trip, the generator light came on. He shook his head in disbelief.

When he stopped at the truck stop, he took a look to see what was wrong. The electrical lines were hooked up and the belt was still turning. He shut the motor off, and it restarted again with no problem, but the warning light was still on. This meant that before long the batteries would be run down, and even though the motor didn't use electricity to run, if it died or got shut down he wouldn't be able to start it without a jump.

So the plan was that he would run until dark, park for the night with the motor running, and continue again in the morning. The only things wrong with this plan were his stoplights, turn signals, marker lights, headlights and license plate light would not be working, but at least he would be traveling almost all freeway.

The next morning he stopped at the truck stop in St. George, Utah, for a cup of coffee and a roll. Knowing that he had no brake lights, he was careful. Sitting at the counter, drinking coffee, the heat of all that had happened seemed to melt away.

When he got back in the truck, the realization of what the real problem was started to dawn on him. As he pulled back on the freeway, he was thinking, *The problem is this truck. The poor old thing has literally been beat to death, and it wouldn't matter who drove it—it would still break down the same. When I get back I'm going to go in and talk to the owner. We still might be able to work things out.*

The very moment he had convinced himself of this, he heard the snap of metal breaking, and the front of the truck wobbled from side to side. This brought his complete attention back to the present. The snap was the gearshift breaking in two while he was mechanically shifting gears. The wobbling front end was when the shifter broke, and he jerked on the steering wheel with his left hand without meaning to.

He rolled to a stop off the side, still holding the shifter lever. The transmission was in neutral, and the motor was still running. He sat there for a moment and looked at where the lever had broken, six inches up from the floor. He told himself, *I don't believe in omens, but if I did, that would be it. When I get back, if I get back, that will be it.* He could not put the transmission in gear with the stubble of lever that was left.

He went to his tool box and got a large set of vice grips. Adjusting them down tight, he clamped them on to what was left of the lever. It would now shift. The Road Ranger button was still connected by the cable to the broken lever, but it was still easy enough to work. When moving, the only time you use the button is between fifth and sixth gear, and it's not activated until you let up and push down on the fuel pedal.

A few hours later he pulled back into Jason's yard. Red came out and took the mileage off the Hub. Shylo didn't even get out of the truck, but he could hear the yard man on the phone inside the building, saying, "Yes, sir, that trailer just pulled into the yard, and I'll have it over there in a few minutes."

When Red went back in, Shylo pulled around to the middle of the yard and parked. He thought, *When I turn this motor off, they are going to have a hard time trying to start it. If I were a good guy I'd drop the trailer and move the tractor out of the way, or at least leave it running and tell the yard man. But, then again, he knew the truth.* They were going to blame him for everything, so what would the sense be in trying to be a good guy?

He set the brakes and shut the motor off. He took his vice grips, his toolbox and his paperwork and went inside. The yard man went out the door. He handed the paperwork to the accountant.

A moment later, the yard man came back in.

He walked up to Shylo and screamed, "WHAT DID YOU DO TO THAT TRUCK?"

Shylo never realized how big that guy really was until he stood there looking up at him. He didn't answer him but just looked back. Finally, the man turned and went back into the yard.

A few minutes later Red came to the counter and handed him a final check. He looked at the amount on the check, picked up his tool box and, without a word to or from anyone, he left the premises, never to return.

1974
owner operator

CHAPTER ONE

Out of work, with no income or even a prospect, Shylo went to a temporary labor company the next morning after leaving Jason's. He was sent to a produce company to unload trailers. Everyone doing the manual labor was from the temporary labor company. Shylo looked at the three men he was working with. They were all old enough to retire, but still needed an income.

He thought, *I guess its only justice that I should end up here. I used to make fun of and degrade the winos that had to get paid on a daily basis. Even though I don't drink wine, it's only appropriate I should experience the other side of the fence. I won't laugh at them anymore, that's for sure.*

The produce was in cartons, but not loaded on skids. Everything was unloaded with dollies and taken to the appropriate section in the cooled warehouse. The four men worked together in rhythm. Two men stacked while two wheeled. At the next trailer they traded places, since stacking was considered the harder of the two jobs.

The day progressed into the afternoon, and Shylo had to admit to himself the three weak-looking old men were relentlessly working his little hiney into the ground.

During their half-hour lunch they were each given half a cantaloupe to eat. While they sat outside eating, a conventional Peterbilt pulled into the lot to deliver a loaded trailer. When they finished and returned, the driver was arguing with the guy they had reported to.

"I'm not required to back that trailer up to any door, that's your responsibility!" He went stomping out the door to drop the trailer where it was.

The middle-aged balding foreman stood with his hands on his hips and yelled, "I gotta have that trailer backed up to door number ten!"

The four men returned to the trailer they were unloading. When they were through, Shylo walked up to the foreman and asked, "Does that little tractor out front run?"

"Yes."

"I can spot the trailer for you. It's no big deal, really."

The foreman left and, a moment later, showed back up with a set of keys. Shylo started the little gasoline truck and hooked up to the trailer. For a moment he sat and looked at the vehicle model printed on the side of the hood. International Loadstar. He thought, *That one time this must have been just about the only truck made.* The numbered metal seal was cut off, the doors were latched open, and he backed the trailer into door number ten with the back edges pressing into the Styrofoam weatherstripping around the warehouse door. When he stepped back up on the dock, everyone was making a big deal about his ability to back a trailer up, except for one of the temporary labor men, who insisted it was pure luck. He held a twenty dollar bill up and said, "I've got twenty dollars that says you can't do that again!"

Even though this was his first day working as a temporary, Shylo still knew where the old guy was coming from. Temporary laborers tend to exaggerate their ability to the point that it becomes a lie. He looked at the money and realized that was four hours of labor for that old guy.

He told him, "Listen, I won't take your money, but I'll prove it was no accident!"

"Oh no, you'll just pull it up a little ways and then back it in."

"How about if I pull out in the lot, do a figure eight and then back in?"

This met the old guy's approval. "Okay."

Deep inside, Shylo said to himself as he went back out the door, *Oh God, after all that, please let me do this the first time without having to pull up.*

Like he said, he pulled out in the lot, performed a figure eight and backed the trailer back up to the door. Both sides were touching the insulation, and the bottom of the trailer was square against the warehouse. When he stepped back up on the dock, everyone just looked at him in awe. The old man who challenged him asked, "You can drive a truck, but you're working for temporary?"

140

Shylo started to feel guilty; he grinned and tried to explain. "It's not that big a deal, really. It was a short wheelbase tractor and a long wheelbase trailer. You can spot that thing on a dime. A long wheelbase tractor and a short wheelbase trailer is the hardest to back up. You turn the steering wheel and five feet later the trailer reacts."

CHapter Two

He stopped explaining and looked at the old man and everyone listening; his explaining the truth only meant that he knew what he was talking about. Never again did he ever feel more honored than he did by the look of respect on the old man's face.

It was now the end of August in 1974, and Shylo decided not to make any quick decisions about his career. He knew if he went to Kentucky to visit his parents he would end up staying there. He didn't want that, but even worse he didn't want to end up sweeping a warehouse floor for a living. He decided to spend two days looking in the paper and then go to the unemployment office.

That night he called his parents' house and talked to Jim. What Jim had to say was very interesting. The owners of Beehive Transfer had retired and left the business to their sons, Reese Holstead, who was Jim's son, and Troy Holstead, who was John's son. The old equipment and the old ways of doing business were being done away with. In fact, they were even backing owner operators who would sign a contract to pull for Beehive.

Shylo asked, "What are their contracts like?"

"I don't know, but a general contract is based upon a percentage of the gross line haul, depending on what the driver pays for. If he supplies the tractor, its maintance, labor, insurance and fuel, then forty-five to fifty-five percent, considering other cost involved, is a good contract. There is always the hidden cost for a company that never shows up on paper, but then again, the driver has the same problem, so they kind of cancel each other out."

"Well, what's it like working directly for Red Horse Van Lines instead of an agent?"

"Not bad, not bad at all. I answer directly to the chairman of the board, Mr. Moccasin."

"Sounds Indian to me;"

"Full-blooded Cherokee, but that's only the half of it. His first name is Water."

Shylo pronounced the full name, Water Moccasin, and laughed.

Jim remarked. "It's not funny. If you work for the guy, you better not laugh. He says he would no more change the name than he would his heritage."

"I didn't mean to laugh, it just kind of caught me off-guard."

CHAPTER THREE

The next morning, Shylo wandered into the Beehive office and asked, "Who does the hiring now?"

There seemed to be a number of new faces in the building. The girl looked up from her desk and asked why.

"I'd like to put in an application."

"An application for what?"

The girl recognized him from when he worked there before, but didn't say so because she couldn't remember his name. Shylo remembered her, but never did know her name.

"For a driver."

She handed him an application and replied, "If you would like to fill this out, Troy will probably interview you this morning."

A few minutes later he was sitting in front of Troy's desk, answering questions. After he had explained why he had taken another job and then left it too, Troy was very interested in him. When the conversation was over, Shylo was going to return to work at seven the next morning. He would be delivering and picking up trailers from Salt Lake to the Tooele Army Depot. Sometimes the trailers would be reloaded at the depot, and other times they would be returned empty. Then after two months he would go with Troy and order a new truck from the Kenworth dealer. Troy would co-sign for his loan, and Shylo would sign a contract with Beehive Transfer. Shylo knew exactly what he wanted: the twin screw, cab-over, thirteen-speed with a 425 Caterpillar diesel.

The next day Shylo made three trips to the depot and put in nine hours. This turned out to be an average work day. Whatever was on the trailer would unload fast and was generally in small cartons, and the trailer was usually left at the door or spotted to load. Military personnel always did the loading.

By the time fall set in, he had become very accustomed to his routine and the one hour overtime every day. He maintained his one-room apartment and managed to give Mary some money each month for child support. He even made an agreement to let her know in advance when he could pick Dustin up for the evening or overnight. She seemed to be easier to deal with when you didn't have to answer to her.

Her customer service position with First West Airlines was going so well that she now had her own office and a telephone number. Instead of picking up some loser at the local "Do Drop Inn," she was associating with some very prominent people and had a reputable male friend, Derrick Blackwell, a successful attorney.

Shylo didn't complete ordering his truck until the end of November, while Troy was ordering two other trucks for Beehive. They were told not to expect delivery for four to five months. With the winter closing in, Shylo felt like he would rather get it in the spring.

Like he told Troy, "It won't fit under the Christmas tree anyway!"

Troy thought about the one hundred foot Christmas tree that was delivered downtown every year and replied, "You wanna bet!"

CHapter Four

The turkeys flew in on unfettered wings, and the connotation of "not a creature was stirring" grabbed the intent of the young at heart no matter what the age of the muscular organ.

A brief shifting back in months and solar days, and a new number was added to the account of years, January 1, 1975. One month later on February 3, Shylo was twenty-seven years old. Mary's new position with First West Airlines fit right in with her personality. She had managed to stay independent but still progress in a career with a social life. She now had the benefit of unlimited travel to anywhere in the United States for both her and Dustin. Her work week consisted of the standard nine-to-five, Monday through Friday. Five-year-old Dustin spent his days at the day care center and was going to start kindergarten in the coming fall. The relationship with his father was still growing, but it was hard for him to understand why he wasn't a permanent, everyday part of his life. With the unquestioning love of a child, he was eager to be a part of his life. Shylo realized this and made a constant effort to earn this treasured trust. Even as young as little Dustin was, he was still receptive and sensitive to his quality of life.

During this time Mary's relationship with Derrick grew. Derrick was a successful lawyer and the stepbrother of billionaire heiress Jean Rasmusen, whose father, Vernon Rasmusen, had left her as the dominate heir of his fortune in bank accounts, holding companies, investments and a conglomeration of securities that held enough stock in other companies to form the investment company named Vernon Securities.

Jean was a long way from being the richest person in the world, but when a person's value goes over a billon dollars they can no longer be referred to as just a millionaire. Vern started out by buying property between Wyoming and Utah and producing oil. Then he made his fortune grow by investing in the fastest growing markets, such as steel, fast food and transportation. His first wife, Jean's mother, died in 1962, and he remarried a woman with a son. Vern died of cancer in 1969 and left his wife, Rachel Rasmussen, and his stepson, Derrick Blackwell, one of his Salt Lake estates and two million dollars. All the rest of his estates and property and the bulk of his fortune was left to Jean.

Derrick continued going to law school at Harvard and graduated. He retained his father's last name of Blackwell, and opened a law office in Salt Lake City. He was one of the lawyers for Vernon Securities, and a social organizer for all the company events. Rachel had a stroke and passed away in July of 1972. This brought the stepbrother and sister closer together. Derrick was now twenty-eight years old, and Jean was twenty-six years old.

Jean missed her father, who always seemed to have the answer for everything, but most of all she missed the family life that existed between them. She was considered the most eligible single girl in Utah, but seemed to have no interest in having a suitor. She was not bashful about hosting parties or events at her east side estate, but this year she was to busy at other designated events to have her own. This year a large Christmas tree was set up and decorated by the servants in the banquet room of her home, and Jean was the only other person to admire it. Derrick's hobby was skiing, and he would take Mary and Dustin to his lodge in Park City to teach them to ski.

On one of the weekend events, he dropped by Jean's home to introduce Mary to his stepsister. Dustin was captivated by the twenty-seven-inch television in her game room, and sat in front of it, watching cartoons. Mary had to turn it off to get him to leave. A few days later, Jean had a large screen delivered to Mary's house.

Then a couple of weeks later she went by to see it. Dustin showed her how great the television worked, and his new fishing pole that he received for Christmas. She grinned and nodded her head.

"We'll have to go fishing in the mountains this summer. I would love to go with someone like you."

She smiled again and looked at Mary. "Honestly, I wasn't trying to be in any way offensive when I sent the television; he just enjoyed mine so well that I could see no reason why he shouldn't have his own."

147

"Believe me, no offense taken. It's the most expensive gift he ever got, but I don't know who enjoys it the most, him or me!"

Jean stood there admiring her coffee table and end tables. "You know, I've seen a lot of different tables in the world, but I've never seen anything like these. They are original!"

The coffee table had a set of tripod legs that supported three round tops at different heights. The wood was oak, with a semigloss dark walnut finish. The three K-type legs were three inches thick each, connected in the middle to form a tripod stand. Connected to the top of each leg was a fifteen-inch round, hollow top. Oak veneer was on the tops, with intermittent holes in the rounded edge. There was no bottom, but a one-and-a-half-inch thick, permanent attaching plate that allowed each top to spin onto the leg. The two matching end tables were a work of ingenuity. The construction was from three-inch oak with a semigloss dark walnut stain that matched the coffee table. Each table had a self-supportive six-foot leg with a T on top that held three hanging lights and a hanging switch. An independent, square, three-inch frame stood two feet from the floor, with a glass top. Two pyramid-shaped legs supported the front, and the back was on a peg from a support arm on the self-supportive leg. A light controlled by the hanging switch showed through a removable picture at the bottom of the square top under the glass.

Jean asked, "Where did they come from?"

"My ex-husband made them in the garage when we were married. It took him almost two years to design and build in his spare time, but they are original and unique to the world. All of the wood, except the veneer on the table tops, was taken from discarded church pews that were beyond repair."

"That's remarkable—he must do woodwork for a living."

"No, actually, he's a truck driver."

"Give me a break! He designs and builds stuff like that, but he drives a truck for a living?"

"Yep. The last I heard he was buying his own truck and would be a contractor."

"Well, if he ever changes his occupation and starts building tables for a living, I'll buy a set."

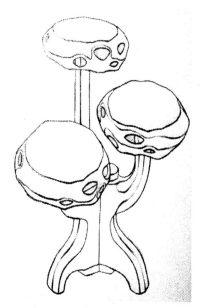

Shylo's custom coffee table

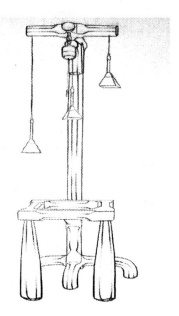

Shylo's custom end table

CHaPTer FiVe

If a Beehive truck was involved in an accident and the tractor was evaluated as totaled out, the company's new agreement with the insurance company was to buy the tractor back (after settlement, sight unseen) at a significantly reduced rate of value. The trailer and the load were different matters altogether. The mechanics would strip that of value from the vehicle and sell the rest to a steel company for recycling. The power train alone could be valued over ten thousand dollars. The power train was seldom damaged in an accident, and if it was, it was always repairable to its original status before the mishap.

Late that January, one of Beehive's oldest drivers, Doyle Mackenzie, wrecked one of their newest tractors in Wyoming. He was on one of the sisters east of Evanston and was killed instantly. The sisters are two mountaintops that look alike. Not only can you see from one top to another, but you can also see all the highway between. That covers a very long distance; twenty miles visibility with no obstacles. Doyle had delivered some new machinery by flatbed to a mall in Rock Springs. Coming back to Salt Lake, he jack-knifed on the wet asphalt coming down the first sister and slid across the median into a truck coming from the opposite direction. The driver was trying to get out of his way, and said it looked like if he could just go a little faster he would be past the oncoming assault. He was hauling a load of heavy gauge, oil field drilling pipe. Doyle's tractor hit the load of pipe head on, just missing the tractor. Doyle's trailer wasn't damaged, but the tractor was totaled out and brought back to Salt Lake City on a goose neck trailer. It set parked in the yard until the crane could unload it.

Early in the morning, Shylo investigated the grim-looking sight. The top driver's side of the cab-over diesel was wiped away like it had been hot butter, down to and including the steering column. He stood on the trailer and looked in through the missing driver's door. A cowboy boot was sitting straight up over where the fuel pedal was. It looked as if the owner could put his foot back into it. He reached over to pick up the boot. He couldn't lift it—with a closer look he could see why. The floorboard was pressed up and around the boot's sole. Holding it in place like metal welded to metal, it looked like the floor was liquid when the boot was set on it and sunk in, then it set up. Shylo quivered at his imagination of what was going on when the force of impact took place. To straighten the jack-knifed unit out, Dole pulled the trailer brake lever down and was pressing so hard on the fuel pedal that he was literally standing up between the steering wheel and the seat. The force of impact was beyond belief and description. Like the small hole left in a sheet of glass from a bullet without shattering the translucent substance.

CHaPTer six

By the end of February, the problems and chill of winter was an everyday event. The mechanics had to deal with frozen air lines, jelled fuel lines and parts breaking because of metal expanding in the cold. The sparkling white of morning frost finally gave way to a warmer climate, as the earth ever so slightly tipped on its axes. The expectation of waiting for his new truck was exhausting for Shylo, and each day seemed to be longer than the one before, but the secret of not exposing this torment was a man thing that only the man was aware of or cared about. The taste of a new lifestyle lay hidden on the horizon, and the knowledge of his capability added up in his day-to-day experience of doing his job. His one room and bathroom apartment was too embarrassing for company, but his only company was Dustin, who never noticed that there were no other rooms. In fact, he seemed to find it entertaining to be able to jump from the couch to the bed. As much fun as this was, it was also dangerous because you might miss the landing pad, so it was prohibited.

CHapTer seven

The brisk morning air of early May hung close to the earth, waiting for the first rays of morning sun to start diluting its density. Once again, the white-capped sentinels of the Wasatch Range stood guard over the valley of Salt Lake. Shylo completed bumping the tires and bleeding the air tanks before jumping up into the loping cab-over. Pressing on the fuel pedal straightened out the rough idling and brought new life to the diesel. With the routine spurt of air from brakes being released, the Beehive Transfer truck headed for the pavement. He looked at the scene in the mirror and then the one in front, and wondered which would make the best painting, with the rustic-looking Union Pacific train station in back or the even more antique horse-drawn freight wagons in front. Sitting in the middle of the large dirt and gravel yard were two stacks of five each, original wood, pioneer freight wagons. They had been stacked with a crane, each one crossways on the other, so the seats and wheels would fit. The weeds growing at the bottom indicated they had been there for some time. The trucks, trailers, bobtails, stake beds, flatbeds and machinery was backed in on each side of the lot. It made a sight that everyone would look at more than once. He remembered the great grandmother of a friend recalling when Beehive delivered freight by horse and wagon to the merchants in Granger a few miles away.

She would say, "It was an all-day trip."

He continued, past the wagons and through the large opening between the office and mechanic shop, when he came to a stop. Backing up so he could see around the parked vehicle he passed, a young black man came back into view, and he stopped. The man had a garden hose, putting water into an airline.

Shylo set the brakes, got out and watched. He stood there with arms folded and a questioning look on his face.

The man finally shook his head no and spoke. "There are no ballast tanks on a trailer?"

Slowly, Shylo shook his head no, and then stuck his hand out. "My name is Shylo Desmond."

Bending the hose to stop the water, he shook his hand and replied, "My name is Lester Anderson."

Lester stepped back, turned the water off and returned to where he was.

Shylo asked, "Who told you to fill those lines with water?"

"His name is Jerry."

Shylo nodded with a look of understanding, and Lester asked, "What! Does Jerry just hate black people?"

"I think Jerry hates everyone. We need to get the water out of that air system. Did you have the motor running at all when you were pouring water into that glad hand?"

"No."

Putting both air hoses on the ground, water drained out of the one. Lester announced, "I'm the new yard man until I learn enough to get a class D chauffeur's license."

Shylo started the motor and released the trailer brake valve. The hot side air line blew water vapor for less than a second. He hooked the glad hands of the hoses to the glad hands on the trailer and replied, "Red is hot, and blue is return."

Then he showed him the small reservoir tank on the trailer and the tractor, and the valve to bleed them.

"If you don't bleed them, water will build up in your system, freeze in the lines during the winter, and your brakes won't release. I've got to go. I'm headed for Tooele Army Depot, but tell me, can you be here a few minutes early in the morning?"

"Why?"

"To get even with Jerry."

Lester shook his head yes and grinned big.

The next morning in the Beehive lot, the loud. frantic scream of a man went through the air. Shylo and Lester ran to the side of Jerry's truck as he was picking himself up off the ground. With urgency, they both asked, "What's wrong?"

As Jerry was standing up straight, he pointed at the open door and shouted "There's a snake in my truck, and it bit me on the ass!"

154

Shylo reached in with one hand and picked up the realistic-looking rattle snake that lay coiled up in Jerry's seat. Holding the rubber replica behind the head and pointing it at Jerry, he laughed and replied, "You know the Jake brake? Well, this is a snake brake, guaranteed to stop anyone!"

Jerry looked at the two advisories for a moment and considered it, but he remained speechless and standing still.

Lester said, "You think we should give it a drink of water? I have a place up there where I fill up all the ballast tanks on the trailers."

Deviously, the two went around the front of Jerry's truck and disappeared.

CHAPTER EIGHT

The first few days of May went by, and Shylo was headed for the yard at the end of the day. He was pulling an empty trailer from Tooele to be parked in the lot. It was five-thirty p.m., and the office closed at five p.m. He would just lock his paperwork in the truck and turn it in to Troy in the morning. Troy was now the boss over twenty-nine men, including four mechanics and a three-man bull gang who specialized in moving heavy items. The dock was still operating with a major upgrade in equipment, and a new foreman, Roy Semen, but only half the men reported to the dock in the mornings. The others reported to Troy, excluding the four mechanics who clocked in and out at the shop next to the office.

Shylo turned off the street into the dirt and gravel lot between the office and the shop. As he straightened the unit out, he could see Troy admiring the three shiny new trucks in the middle of the lot. They had been piggy-backed in from the factory. Piggy-backed is when one or more tractors in succession are mounted by their front axle to the fifth-wheel of another tractor for towing. Shylo's truck was on the end. His was the Aerodyne, and the other two were the standard, double-size sleeper cab-overs.

Troy announced to Shylo as he pulled up next to him, "Sharp looking, aren't they?"

"Yeah, there's a lot of money there too."

"Tell me about it. My names on the bottom line for all three, and yours is the only one that's been sold. I have to find buyers for the other two. I'm sure glad we changed the company colors from military green to red. The new

156

delivery trucks at the dock are red. Otherwise these would be the only red vehicles here."

Troy planned to turn all the equipment red in the future. Shylo hurried and spotted his unit and then returned to join Troy.

"I don't mean to brag, but mine is the best looking one there."

"It should be. Yours cost eighty thousand and the other two cost fifty thousand each."

Shylo was only the third person to sign an agreement as owner operator for Beehive. The other two had bought used company trucks. They were nice vehicles, but they were still used and dark green in color. These men would be given first option at buying a newer truck and trading back the old ones. If they were not interested, then the vehicles would sit in the lot, open for inspection and a test drive to Beehive drivers that might be interested in becoming owner operators under the Beehive dispatch.

Shylo walked around his truck, touching it.

Troy replied, as he got ready to leave, "The mechanics will set it down in the morning. Not only is it the best looking truck here, but I'll bet it's the most powerful with that big, dark yellow Caterpillar motor."

He left, and Shylo looked at what was visible of the diesel motor, from the front end being up in the air. The distinctive dark yellow was customary for Caterpillar. Of course, it would be the most expensive to have worked on, but it would be worth the money to satisfy his vain ego when he passed the other trucks going uphill. He had signed a good contract with the bank to pay for it; nineteen percent on five years. The contract with Troy was equally as good. A five-year contract at fifty-five percent of the gross line haul.

Shylo paid for the truck, the insurance, the fuel, any expenses for labor to load or unload, and all of his own expenses, such as meals and lodging.

Like Troy said, "I do want you to be able to make those truck payments."

The following morning it was hard to leave the yard and go to Tooele, but he had an idea of the anguish he would suffer to watch his truck being set down. Troy grinned at him.

"Don't worry, I'll be standing there when they set it down."

He was back in the lot by ten a.m., and it was still sitting there.

Again he left and was back by lunch. It was sitting on the ground with the door unlocked. He spent the next half-hour inspecting the red diamond pleated interior, the sleeper area and the rest of the truck.

Troy walked over after returning from lunch and said, "They still have the batteries to put in and a couple other things to put on. You may as well make that last trip to Tooele. If you stayed here you would only be waiting for nothing. Tomorrow morning you can drop it off at the paint shop for lettering. It will be there all day, and then the next day you have an appointment to take it back to the dealer. They have a representative to show you everything about it and answer your questions."

The next morning was a day of excitement. He took his first drive in his new truck. Driving something that nice made it worth living in a one-room apartment. The transmission was tight but still shifted like it knew what you wanted it to do. The hollow sound of the twin exhaust excited the senses while the high-pitched twirling of the turbo chimed in to do back-up in this band of sounds. The smell of the new leather caused the nose to drink deeply of this intoxicating odor and excited the taste buds. The look of perfection captured the eyesight and created a desire to touch the vehicle's beauty.

That night he called Mary and made an appointment to pick Dustin up the next night and go for a ride. The following day the Kenworth representative showed him everything he needed to know about the truck. He spent the entire day familiarizing himself with the vehicle.

That evening he picked up Dustin and drove him around in the truck. Eventually, setting him in his lap, he let him help turn the steering wheel.

CHaPTer nine

The next day he hauled his first load. It was a short trip to Elko, Nevada, with a large load of cement pipe for highway construction, and he came back empty. He didn't even get to break-in the sleeper.

The following day he found himself pulling a full trailer of used telephone equipment to Denver, Colorado, and returning with rebuilt parts. This was a three-day trip with unloading and reloading.

Twice he made this trip, and then he took a full load of machinery parts for oil field rigs into Texas. Then he hauled a load of nuts and bolts and other attachment items to Colorado, and a load of wood products back to Salt Lake City. Shylo had a quick overnight at home, just long enough to visit Dustin and take him for another ride. The following day he took the truck to the Kenworth dealer for its five thousand mile checkup.

The Jake brake had to be repaired, and it spent all day in the shop. It actually had three Jake brakes, a quarter, a half and a three-quarter. The Jake brake causes coordinating cylinders to pre-ignite, using the compression of these pistons to slow the vehicle down. On an eight cylinder motor, a quarter Jake is two pistons; a half is four; and a three-quarter is six. It works electrically, delivering a spark on the compression stroke before the piston reaches top dead center and causes the vehicle to slow down.

When it was ready, he picked it up and went back to Beehive's lot. Lester stopped him as he pulled in. "Hey, something that ugly is supposed to use the back entrance."

"Yeah, you be a good boy. I'll let you ride in it someday for fifty cents."

"But momma only gives me twenty-five cents a week."

"Well, start saving your quarters, little boy, 'cause fifty cents only buys a sixty-second ticket anyway."

"What happens after sixty seconds and the ride ain't over?"

"I don't know, I haven't had any paying customers yet."

He grinned at Lester as he continued into the lot to park. Sliding into the saddle of the new work horse filled Shylo's agenda. He never knew what was next until he finished what he was doing. The trips kept lasting longer, and the destinations were further away.

1977
THE FIre VICTIM

CHAPTER ONE

One Monday morning the phone rang in the little office of the Southern Baptist church on Ray Street in Magna, Utah.

"Reverend John Franklin Goodwin here, how may I help you?" Using a marker for his place, he closed the Bible. A long pause came from the other end. The reverend was a well-seasoned servant of God, who had no trouble speaking to anyone, but knew when to keep his mouth shut and listen. A few more moments went by, and he could hear the unmistakable sound of someone trying to regain their composure.

He could hear the wet, nasal sound; the shortness of breath; and then one large gulp of air before the voice at the other end finally blurted out the loud words, "He wants to talk to you!"

"Who?"

"I'm sorry, my husband is a driver for Beehive Transfer, and he was in a real bad explosion at a plant in Idaho while making a delivery. They flew him back to Salt Lake City, Utah, to the burn center at the Delta Hospital. He wants to be saved before he dies. His name is Jerry Williams. He'll probably be dead before you get here, but I wish you would come anyway."

"That place is clear across the valley, but I'll be as quick as I can. It's going to take some time. Wait, where is the burn center?"

"You know where the main building is?"

"Yes."

"Just come in the front door and follow the signs to the burn center. I'll be waiting. Thank you!"

The reverend wrote a quick note that he placed on the center of his desk: "Be back later. Went to Delta Hospital. Rev. Goodwin."

He rushed out the door, and thirty-five minutes later he parked in the sub-level parking and hurried to the front entrance. Inside, the information boards, hanging from the ceiling much like the ones in an airport, contained all locations. The burn center was the fourth floor. He stepped off the main elevator on the fourth floor, not knowing which way to turn, and spotted the signs with arrows. Severe burns to the right. He hurried down the corridor and saw a lady standing in a flower print dress. She seemed to have tuned out the world as she searched in vain for a dry spot on her handkerchief.

He walked up to her and said, "Mrs. Williams?"

Slowly, she looked at his Bible and then up at his face. The reverend looked into her large red eyes that literally seemed to be floating in pools of water. If she tried to speak, she was just going to lose it again. So for the briefest of moments, she looked back, while the pools overflowed and etched down the lower eye lids, over the cheekbone and down off the chin.

She then turned and walked across the hall. He followed her into a large waiting room that connected to another hall on the other side. To the immediate left was a counter that stretched between two walls. Behind it was a variety of shelves and doors, and two females dressed in white nurse uniforms.

Halfway across the room, Mrs. Williams stopped. Faltering, she put her left hand on the counter. Quickly, a girl behind the counter grabbed her arm and asked, "Are you okay?"

The reverend assisted her to a large chair as the other girl behind the counter went out a door and came around with a glass of water. The nurse asked, "Do you need a doctor, ma'am?"

"No."

The reverend said softly, "Sit here and try to drink some water."

The nurse left, and he returned to the counter and retrieved the Bible he had laid down. The girl sat behind the counter, looking at him. He acknowledged, "I'm here to see Jerry Williams."

"Are you family?"

"No, I'm Reverend John Goodwin."

She reached under the counter and took out a white gown, a hair cover, a paper mask and a visitor tag. With a magic marker, she wrote 418 in the round blank spot on the tag, peeled off the back and attached it to the front of the gown. Handing this to him, she pointed to the large opening.

"Go through that door and wait for the doctor."

He slipped the gown on and went through the opening to find the doctor waiting for him. The doctor stood there all in white, with his arms wrapped around a clipboard, looking at the reverend. He looked back as the doctor continued to stare in his face.

The doctor said, "Do we need the Bible?"

"Yes, sir, it's part of my armor. The breast plate of righteousness, the shield of faith, the helmet of salvation, and the sword of God, his word."

This would at least make others smile, but not so with the good doctor. People in the medical profession are trained to have a look of non-compassion for their own benefit, but the doctor's look came from a person who had witnessed more than he should ever see. Hurriedly, John searched underneath the gown for a church schedule in his shirt pocket.

He handed it to him and said softly, "Please come to church. I would be honored with your presence."

He took the card, nodded down the hall with his head and said, "The first door on your right, keep the mask on, and only one visitor at a time, please!"

The reverend slowly walked down the hall, opened the door and walked in. The room was empty except for an elevated lattice, supported by a wood frame in the middle of the floor. He quietly shut the door and walked over to the lattice. Being a veteran of heavy combat for two years, and a minister of over twenty years, he had seen some horrible sights, but this one made him forget everything. The body, tied to the lattice, looked like large strips of burnt bacon. You couldn't tell if it was clothes melted to the person, or just naked, burnt skin. The fusion of fire made the shoes a permanent part of the feet. The head was burnt beyond recognition. The hair was gone, the ears were gone, the eyelids were burnt shut, the nose was gone and the mouth was an empty hole with a tongue that still existed.

John looked with disbelief and mental pain, while he thought, *How do I tell if he's alive?*

Too afraid to touch him for a pulse, he leaned over his head, looking for some evidence of life. A teardrop fell and hit the blackened face hard on the cheek. John flinched at what he had done.

The words were muffled and horse, but understandable. "I...don't...want...to...go...back!"

"Go back where?"

"To hell!"

A long pause filled the room while the reverend gathered his wits. This was his job, bringing souls to Christ, and he knew the importance of this. Every time Jesus saved a soul their name was added to the eternal book of life, and they didn't go to hell.

Still leaning forward, John said very humbly, "As it is written in the Bible, only Jesus can save you. This redemption is free, all you have to do is ask, knowing that you commit your soul to him."

"Jesus…save me."

One last small, satisfying breath, and then there was nothing. The tears started to stream down the good reverend's face, and he had no desire to restrain them.

Slowly he got up and walked out the door. Mrs. Williams was in the hall with a younger couple. Taking the hair net and mask off, he walked up to her. With tears in his eyes, and a smile on his face, he reported, "He got saved!"

1977
LOVE'S FIRST BITE

CHAPTER ONE

The fresh morning air felt good as Shylo walked from his sleeper to the cafe in the truck stop. It was on the outskirts of Kansas City, Kansas, and in the direction of home. He was fully loaded with canned corn products for Salt Lake City. A flat tire on the trailer had forced him to stop there. He would arrange to have the tire fixed first, and then shower and eat before he reported in on the watts line. With business completed, he called the number.

"Hello, Troy, this is Shylo. I was loaded at the cannery yesterday but ended up with a flat tire on the trailer. How's everything going?"

"Fine. When do you expect to be back?"

"It depends on this tire. It will probably be the day after tomorrow."

"I just wanted to tell you, remember yesterday when I told you about Jerry being in that fire in Idaho?"

"Yes."

"He died."

A long silence came over the phone, and Shylo said, "He must have been burnt pretty badly."

"Yeah. I didn't see him, but I understand he was burnt beyond belief."

"Well, include me in on the flowers from Beehive, and I'll talk to you tomorrow."

CHAPTER TWO

Mary asked Derrick as they sat down to eat, "Why does Jean want to take Dustin and me fishing?"

"She said she promised Dustin to take him fishing in the mountains."

"Where your condo is?"

"No, where her house is. Actually, she owns some land up there with a river running through it."

"It must be nice to have money!"

"You don't know the half of it. She has a twenty-four hour bodyguard service that watches her from the background unless she travels, and then they usually travel with her."

"As rich as she is, I don't blame her."

"I don't either, but it was her father who set the bodyguard service up, and she just kept it that way."

"I have a question. If she was kidnaped, who would get the ransom note?"

Derrick laughed as he thought about it. "That's a very good question. To be honest, she's the only one there is that could settle a ransom demand, so she would have to get the note. If that was to happen, I would help her all I could. Anyway, she'll be contacting you to make arrangements to go. Don't worry about buying fishing poles or anything to take; it will already be there."

CHAPTER THREE

"Okay, gang, enough of this hardcore fishing life. It's time we got the breakfast we missed this morning." Jean looked to see if Dustin and Mary approved as she pulled into the cafe at Kimball Junction off of Interstate 80. They had been to Jean's house all day Saturday, fishing, and had decided to come back Sunday morning. Dustin and Jean had been arguing over who caught the biggest fish; trouble was, they let the fish go without measuring them. All the same, if one was larger you could have only told by measuring it. So, the exaggeration of how big those fish were kept growing between them. Mary, who thought everyone knew she caught the biggest one, kept her mouth shut.

Meanwhile, as they entered the parking lot, Shylo entered Interstate 80 westbound from the highway. It felt good to him to be on the spacious freeway and off that narrow highway. The scenery was worth the drive, but after a while the micro-judging behind the steering wheel started to get on your nerves. Navigating with just a little room on this side and a little room on that side of the vehicle could wear you out. The early morning twilight had since become daylight, and he felt the need for food. He knew just the place, the cafe at Kimball Junction.

The fluttering noise of a three-quarter Jake brake broke the air as the truck rolled to a stop in front of the cafe. Mary's mouth dropped open as she watched the semi from her table.

"Oh my word, it's Shylo!" She turned and looked at Dustin. "You just sit right here and ignore him, young man. It's bad enough to deal with Mr. Macho at home. I have no desire to confront him in public, like two old friends at the store."

Jean looked at Mary across the table with a grin. "Well, well, I'm going to get to see the truck driver who should have been a carpenter. I'd like to know why you got a divorce. I know you didn't meet Derrick until later."

"Well, I'll tell you what. It's impossible for two to be as one when they're as different as night and day. I've got nothing against him, but I didn't realize I had nothing for him until after we got married."

Shylo opened the front door and walked in. Looking at the "Please Seat Yourself" sign, he turned to the right to a booth in front of the windows and sat down facing away from Mary's table. The waitress walked over, put a glass of water and a menu on the table and said, "I'll be back in a minute."

Shylo looked in the menu for a moment and then opened his logbook and started writing. The waitress showed back up and stood there with pen and pad in hand. "What's special?"

"It's all special. It just depends what you want to eat."

He grinned and looked up. "Let me reword that. What's good to eat?"

"The special. Ham, sausage or bacon, and eggs with biscuits and gravy."

"Well, you see, the problem is, I never did eat last night, so I need two meals. Let's try two specials, one with sausage and one with bacon, eggs scrambled, and coffee."

She finished writing and said, "You got it."

She took the menu and promptly left. He returned to filling out his logbook.

Mary looked at Jean, saying nothing, but Jean conceived the words in Mary's thoughts and replied, "I don't care who came in and sat down, I'm not going anywhere until I eat!"

A man, a woman and a little girl were seated at a table in back of the room. Everyone seemed content at their own business when the front door opened and in walked a girl and three motorcycle riders. The girl was in front and walking at a fast pace to stay ahead of the ragged-looking, unshaven men. She went to the center of the room and sat down at the counter. She was glad to be in a public place. The three men joined her; they had been trying to force her off the road for some time when she pulled into the cafe and hurried in.

The girl looked at the waitress behind the counter and asked, "Can I get a sweet roll and a glass of milk?"

The waitress looked at the largest of the three men, who seemed to be the leader. He laughed and replied, "Yeah, let's have sweet rolls and milk all around."

She retrieved four rolls and four milks for the customers. The men continued to insult the girl. Shylo looked up with his eyes and then with his head at the waitress, who was sitting plates of food on his table.

He asked her, "What are you looking at?"

For a moment the girl looked back, very straight lipped, as if she was trying to out-stare him. Then she turned and left to retrieve more coffee. He finished his logbook while listening to what was going on at the counter. He looked at the food with desire, made a small groan and tasted the gravy with his finger as he rose from the table. Looking at the waitress and speaking in a matter-of-fact tone, he said, "Breathe on this and keep it warm, okay!"

He turned and walked toward the people at the counter. The leader, who was watching him come over, said to the others, "Oh my goodness, what do we have here?"

Shylo walked up to the large man, who was now grinning at him, and spit in his face. He immediately retaliated with a big right fist, sending Shylo spreadeagle face-down on a sweet roll. Shylo grinned, looked up at the girl who was being harassed, and said, "I hate it when that happens!"

The other two bikers grabbed him by the arms and turned him around to face his advisory. The girl, seeing her opportunity, ran out the door to leave. As Shylo was swung around, his right foot came up, striking his opponent hard in the groan. His heel immediately came down hard on the foot of the man holding his right arm. When the man let go to grab his hurt foot, Shylo's right fist met the guy to his left squarely in the nose. The men on each side of him ran out the door. He grabbed the arm of the one in front and twisted it behind his back, forcing his head down on the counter. He held the arm with his left hand, took a fork with his right hand, and pressed the prongs into his neck. Shylo whispered in his ear, "I think you owe the lady an apology."

The man's eyes went back and forth, searching for the girl. Shylo pressed harder on the fork. The waitress, who was now behind the counter, screamed at the sight of blood coming from his neck.

Hysterically, he started repeating, "I apologize! I apologize!"

Shylo took the fork from his neck and threw him against the counter. He reached for the small bleeding holes in his throat, but Shylo knocked his arms away and stood holding the fork like a real weapon. The frightened man braced himself against the counter, not knowing what was going to happen. Shylo eased his rigid stance and reached for a paper napkin. Spitting in the center of the napkin, he wiped the blood from the guy's neck, folded the paper and stuffed it in the guy's shirt pocket. Stepping to one side, he informed the now ill-fated person, "Maybe you should leave before the cops show up."

This didn't have to be repeated. He took off at a run to vacate the premises. Reaching the front door, he paused, turned around, pointed his finger at Shylo and said, "I'll get even with you!"

Shylo, still holding the fork, bent forward and ran at him like a football player making a tackle. The troublemaker bolted out the door, and Shylo stopped about halfway, laughing at his own actions. His laugh abruptly ended, and he stumbled in the process of stopping as a child's voice said, "Hi, Daddy!"

His son, who was sitting at a table, was almost close enough to touch. Totally surprised, he held his hand up waist high and greeted his son.

"Hi, buddy."

"Buddy" had always been his nickname for Dustin. Mary took the five-year-old by the arm and repeated what she had said earlier, "I told you to keep quiet!"

Shylo backed away with a confused look and went back to his own table. Picking up his logbook, he placed some money with the uneaten food and, in a matter of moments, he was going down the asphalt one gear at a time.

Jean looked across the table at Dustin with affection and understanding. She asked, "Does your dad ever come to visit you?"

"Sometimes. He has to let Mom know when he's taking me, but then I get to drive his new truck."

"I don't know, that truck looked awfully big to me."

"It is. It's a 'K Whopper.'"

"A what?"

"That's what drivers call a Kenworth."

With a questioning look, Jean smiled and asked, "Does 'K Whopper' mean both the truck and trailer?"

"Nope, it just stands for the truck. If it was a Peterbilt it would be called a 'Big Dick.'"

Her mouth fell open as she lowered her head and replied, "Give me a break! I think your dad is a bad influence on you!"

"He's not the one who gave them those names. That's what they're called by other drivers."

"Oh, well, that's okay then."

He grinned, and the size of the fish argument was forgotten. His smile conceded that he liked having Jean for a friend.

That evening, the phone rang at Shylo's place.

"Hello."

"Hi. You don't know me, but I'm Jean, Mary's friend, and I want to invite you to bring Dustin up to my place tomorrow night to watch the Fourth of July fireworks. I live way up on the east side, and from the patio above my garage you can see all the lights in the valley. I'm the person that was with them today at the cafe. We'll have a barbecue before dark, and then watch the show in the valley. I invited Mary, but she already had plans."

"I'll have to get permission from Mary to bring Dustin."

CHAPTER FOUR

The next evening Shylo drove up to the front of Jean's estate. He got out and pressed the button under the speaker box.

"Can I help you?"

"Shylo and Dustin, we're expected by Jean."

He had used his tractor, without the trailer, to pick up his son and go to Jean's. He watched the large gate slide open, and the remote camera on top pointed straight at him. He got back in the truck, drove in and parked to the side in the two-lane circular driveway. He asked Dustin as they walked up to the door, "Are we supposed to ring the door bell or knock?"

"I don't know."

Before reaching the two large front doors, one opened and an older gentleman invited them in. He escorted them to a library room and told them to have a seat. Jean would be with them momentarily.

A few moments later, Jean arrived at the front door in a limousine. The driver opened the door, and she stepped out. The servant opened the front door, and she went in.

She asked, "Did Shylo and Dustin show up?"

"They got here a few minutes after you called; they're in the library waiting for you."

She stepped into the library and said, "I'm sorry, I hope you haven't been waiting long. I'm Jean."

Shylo looked at the beautiful young blonde who walked up to greet them. She wore a tight-fitting white blouse with a dark miniskirt and high-heeled sandals. The scent of her perfume filled the room like the smell of a rose garden. Her long white legs and red fingernails and toenails would make a little boy raise his eyebrows and look twice—even when he didn't know why he was looking.

"Hi, my name is, uh, Shylo. Yeah, that's my name. I remember it because that's what everybody calls me." He grinned.

She shook his hand and grinned. Dustin stuck out his hand and said, "Wow, you must be a model."

She shook his hand and smiled. "How's my fishing partner? I was gonna change for the evening, but after a compliment like that, I don't think I will."

She turned and looked at Shylo, whose head jumped back to an eye level position. "Shall we go up to the patio above the garage? There's a barbecue waiting for us there, and I haven't eaten all day. If I know Renee, the cook, there's everything from pheasant under glass to ribs up there. All the people who work here at this house will be there."

"How many people work here?"

"Five. I have one cook, one housekeeper, one chauffeur, one security man and one yard man. They all worked for my father, and they're very much a part of this estate. I'd hate to have to replace one of them."

"Well, if one of them ever quits, let me put in an application."

She looked at him and grinned.

On top of the garage was a large flat roof, converted into a fenced-in deck. The south and west side overlooked the valley. On the north side was a large grill with buffet tables on each side. A heavenly smell filled the air and made the mouth water for a taste of the delicious odor. They walked up to a table and sat down. Another older gentleman, who seemed to hold his arms at military attention, walked up to the table.

"Miss Jean, there is steak, chicken, a salad with king crab, deviled eggs, potato salad, baked beans and hot rolls. What can I get you?"

"Renee, it all looks very good. I want you to be the first to get a plate so everyone will know it's ready. We will serve ourselves."

"Very well, ma'am."

He grinned and turned to go eat. Jean looked at Shylo and replied, "Actually, these are the best people in the world. I don't hesitate to call them my family."

He looked long and deep into the blue eyes of the woman who had caused him to forget his name for a brief moment and stutter like a fool. A soft summer breeze blew a lock of golden hair around the side of her face, and his mind went blank again. Quickly, he fumbled through the memory in his brain to come up with what she had said. Oh yeah, family—requires no answer.

He spoke softly as he looked in her eyes, "Windy up here, isn't it?"

She moved her chair back from the table. "Lets get something to eat, I'm starved!"

They followed her toward the food. Shylo watched her walk, putting one foot in front of the other. He thought, *I'm going to have to force myself to eat; I've lost my appetite.* Then he reasoned to himself. *I've got to stop this; it's like looking in a storefront window at something I'll never have. I won't look at her.*

"Shylo?"

He looked up and replied softly to her request. "Yes."

"Dustin said he drives your big truck."

Their plates were now full, and they wandered back to their table.

"That's right. He sits up in my lap and drives that thing like a professional."

Dustin set his plate on the table and, with a smile, looked at Jean.

She smiled. "Well, that's not fair. I wanna drive too."

Dustin went back to get the drinks, and Shylo hurried to assist Jean sitting down. Then he sat down and asked, "Could I sit in your lap?"

Very softly, very honestly and very matter-of-fact, he replied, "You could sit wherever you want."

Her eyebrows rose, and she smiled with approval at the man who was causing her heart to quicken since she first laid eyes on him two days ago. Dustin returned, and they continued to eat. After a few minutes, he realized that she couldn't keep her eyes off of him, anymore than he could keep his eyes off of her. Dustin forged through the delicious food without hesitation.

The evening progressed, and Shylo was captured by the conversation of this beautiful girl who spoke, and even the wild birds would listen. He sat starring into her deep crystal, hazel blue eyes, and realized that she was waiting for his answer, but he didn't know what she had said. "I'm sorry, what did you say?"

"I asked how long you have been a truck driver."

"My father was a driver, and I followed him."

He looked around and couldn't see Dustin. "Where did Dustin go?"

"The game room. Would you like to see it? We have at least an hour before it gets dark."

Without question, he followed her to a large game room, complete with

178

pinball machines, a bowling alley and a professional pool table. Dustin was busy at a full-size skeet ball game. Jean opened a door, looked at Shylo and said, "Come with me."

They stepped into the inside of the garage. Thirty cars were lined up in the large garage.

He looked at the vehicles; some older, some newer; but they all looked like they were sitting on the showroom floor. A white with red interior '62 Corvette convertible caught his eye.

"Wow!"

She looked at him and smiled. "Would you like to drive it?"

"Well, of course."

"Well, just a minute. I'll get the key and tell Dustin we'll be back in a moment."

Forty-five minutes later he backed the car back into its spot in the garage. Once it was in place, he turned the motor off, handed her the key and smiled.

"I'll repeat what I said earlier. Wow!"

She smiled and took the keys. "I tell you what, anytime you want to drive it, just come over and we'll go for a ride."

His smile went to a straight face. "You sure got a lot of trust for someone you don't know."

She opened her door and proceeded to get out. "Just because I let you drive my car doesn't mean I trust you."

He hurried around the vehicle to assist her. Too late, she was shutting the door. He asked, "How am I ever going to impress you if you won't let me?"

She smiled, and her eyebrows went up again. "Do I impress you?"

He stood straight and looked at her feet in the high-heeled sandals, then slowly up her body and stopped at her eyes. He sighed and said, "Yes."

"Well, let me tell you a deep, dark secret. I've been told that half the eligible men in this state are trying to impress me, but you're the only one who's ever driven my favorite car."

Carefully, he placed his finger under her chin and leaned forward to taste the nectar of her succulent, full, red lips. Her heart was beating so fast that when his lips touched hers she felt weak enough to faint. She had to put her arms around his shoulders to keep from falling. After a moment of groaning with agonizing pleasure, they separated and backed away. Not saying a word, but knowing they had experienced the sting of love's first bite, she went into the game room, and he followed. Dustin was still playing skeet ball and didn't really want to leave, but the idea of seeing all the fireworks in the valley got his attention.

They returned to the patio over the garage. Slowly they wandered along the west side of the top, looking at the lights of the valley increase while the daylight faded. The patio had been cleaned up, and the employees of the house with their relatives were there to watch the show. Shylo stuck his hand out to greet the person in front of him. "Hello, my name is Shylo."

"And my name is Renee. It's a pleasure to meet you. Is that your pretty red truck in the driveway?"

"Yes, it is. It's a Kenworth."

"Do you work for Kenworth?"

Shylo grinned and dropped his head. "I'm afraid not, sir. I'm just a dumb truck driver who owes the bank half of his life for the next five years to pay for that bright red toy."

Suddenly, a large ball of light exploded in the center of the valley, emitting a perfect circular pattern of smaller lights. A few moments later more spectacular views of fireworks were displayed, capturing everyone's attention and emotions. Shylo felt someone holding his right hand. Dustin was on his left side, so he looked to his right hand. He followed the hand to the arm, and then to Jean's face. She was looking at him with an expression that seemed to say, "If you don't want me holding your hand, let me know now." Very softly, and twice as gently, he clutched her hand and looked deep into her eyes with the desperate look of a very lonely person.

The fireworks lasted for over an hour and climaxed with a fountain of various cascading lights from the sky to the ground. The show ended, and Dustin ambled back to the game room.

One by one, everybody said goodnight and retired to their space. They were left alone, looking at the lights of the city.

He remarked, "It was a great evening."

"Yes, one I'm not going to forget."

Gently, she put her finger under his chin and leaned up to kiss his lips. His hands wandered from her sides to her back, while the intoxicating taste of her lips made him drunk with the lust for her body. Again, they slowly separated, knowing this wasn't the place.

She grinned at him and asked, "Would you like to work for Kenworth?"

"And I bet you could make it happen, huh?"

"Well, probably not, but who would want to when a better opportunity exists."

He grinned and shook his head. "How do you know I don't abuse the opposite sex?"

"Yeah, I've seen how you treat the opposite sex. You protect them. I've seen how you treat people when you're not trying to put on a show for anyone. You treat them like you would want them to treat you. You impress me when you're not trying to. Besides that, you turn me on."

His smile was gone, and his face was very serious. He put the tip of his index finger on her nose and whispered, "You have a way of making my insides melt, and I act like a fool in front of you."

Looking at each other for a moment, they turned and went down to the game room. Dustin had gone back to the skeet ball game. He grinned and spoke out, while picking up a wooden ball, "They used to call me a hustler back in the old days."

Jean retaliated to his statement. "Give me a break! Your 'old days' was sucking on a nipple and pumping up a diaper! I could beat you any day of the week, and twice on Sunday."

He smiled and remarked while he played, "If you talk the talk then you gotta walk the walk."

Her mouth fell open as she looked at Shylo.

He grinned and shook his head. "Don't look at me. I have no idea who that child is."

With her eyebrows raised, she pointed at him and said, "I'll take you up on that challenge, just not tonight. We decided to make popcorn and watch Nightmare Theatre."

"That sounds fun, can I watch too?"

"Only if you turn the TV on while we get the popcorn."

She went to the kitchen, and Shylo followed. He stopped after going through the doorway. She turned and asked, "Is something wrong?"

"No. I'm just looking. The average house isn't as large as your kitchen."

She grinned and replied, "The dining room is twice as large, with running water."

Handing him two bags of microwave popcorn with plastic bowls, she opened three bottles of pop. Then they returned to the television in the game room. Shylo sat on the couch, across from Dustin's couch, and put the drinks on the coffee table. Jean put one bag of popcorn in the microwave against the wall and returned to sit next to Shylo.

On the TV, Godzilla was being awakened by a nuclear blast. Dustin was grinning at the movie when he glanced at the two across from him. Slowly, his grin dissipated, and his eyes returned to look at them. Funny how those things will dawn on a child with the snap of a finger. She had taken her sandals off, and he had his arm around her. They had their eyes glued to the TV, as if they had no knowledge that Dustin was there. For a short while he observed with a somber face, like a decision of approval or disapproval was taking place. Then he stretched out on the sofa and returned to the movie while his votes were being counted. Godzilla was jumping up and down, waving his little arms, swishing his big tail, breathing fire and shaking the earth because he had been woken up.

Five minutes later, Dustin was sound asleep. Clutching Shylo's hand, Jean stood up, and he followed. She picked up her shoes and looked at Dustin.

"I'll come back and put a sheet over him."

She turned the volume down on the TV, and they went across the house to her bedroom.

1977
THE LOVE AFFAIR

CHAPTER ONE

Lester walked by Shylo, who was on a short ladder, cleaning his windshield next to Beehive's mechanic shop. He stopped walking to speak.

"Well, well, well. If it isn't old what's-his-name, driving the old what's-this-thing."

Grinning from ear to ear, Shylo turned to look, and Lester remarked, "You look like the cat that ate the canary."

Shylo's grin grew even larger. "So, how's the big truck driver doing?"

"If I had something like this to drive, I guess I'd be grinning from ear to ear too."

"You know, you're on the wrong road. In the right lane, but definitely on the wrong road. The glorious life of trucking is not what it seems to be."

He stopped grinning to become serious. "Honestly, man, if you're a little boy or just getting into it, it seems bigger than life. But sooner or later you realize there's a lot more to life than devoting it to such a thankless, hardcore profession."

Lester's rebuttal was both statement and question. "You seem happy enough."

Shylo's ear-to-ear grin returned. "I got a girlfriend."

"Oh, I see."

"No, you don't see. This girl isn't just special, she's superior!"

"Superior to what?"

"To any other girl."

"Daddy told me that in the dark they all feel the same."

"Well, Daddy was wrong, Hoss. The superior ones can jumpstart your heart just by holding your hand."

"You sound like a country song."

"No, just your friendly neighborhood love counselor."

"Well, the Love Machine needs no counseling, and that's what Mrs. Love Machine says. So, if you're cleaning your windshield, you must be en route for somewhere."

"Las Vegas."

"What's in Las Vegas?"

"Two fun-filled days and nights with a superior person."

Shylo set the short ladder and water bucket next to the shop. With a gesture of goodbye to his friend, he continued to take the truck and hook up to a trailer in the yard. Lester went into the shop. For a few months now he had obtained a class D chauffeur's license and was learning how to drive. But his job also involved being a gopher for mainly the mechanics, who always needed some kind of an errand run. But working with them proved to provide the best training he could get.

He stepped back out the shop door and looked in the direction where Shylo was. The lower part of his mouth dropped open, and he put his hands on his hips. A long black limousine had stopped in front of Shylo's unit, and Shylo opened its back door for a blonde girl to get out. Meanwhile, the chauffeur had retrieved a suitcase and overnight bag out of the trunk. For a moment, Shylo stood looking at Jean, who was wearing red crushed velvet boots, Levi's and a pink blouse.

"You look absolutely superior!"

He was wearing a white shirt with black Levi's and black boots.

She looked in his eyes. "I could say the same for you, but I don't think you need to be told."

He put her luggage up in the truck while she dismissed her driver, then he assisted her getting in. She bounced up and down in the seat. "Air ride seats. I've never been in a limousine that had that luxury."

He showed her where the adjusting lever for the seat was as the long black car pulled away. Then he closed her door and turned to get in. He stopped and looked toward the shop where Lester was still standing, about half a football field away. He held his right thumb up in the air, and Lester shook his head no. He finished getting in and looked at his passenger.

"Are we ready to go?"

"Absolutely."

"Well, let's make a mile then."

With the silver button down and the splicer in low, he put the gear shift in second, pushed in on the two brake valves and let out on the clutch. The silver trailer, which had been part of a line of trailers, was now part of his unit that was pulling away. Jean watched everything with enthusiasm and said, "It looks so much bigger on the inside than you would think from the outside."

He grinned and glanced at her while going through the gears. "I hate this dirt lot. It always messes up a clean wash job."

"They should pave it."

"I hope they have that in mind for some day, but I rather doubt it."

They pulled onto the asphalt, and she grinned like an excited little girl. "What's in the trailer?"

"I don't know." He held up his shoulders. "All I know is it's not perishable or hazardous. The trailer was loaded and sealed at Tooele Army Depot; we deliver it to Ellis AFB, and they will spend one day unloading and another reloading it. Then, we pick it up and bring it back to Salt Lake to be delivered back to the Tooele Depot." He glanced at her with a grin. "It wouldn't surprise me if it's loaded with new pre-stamped, top-secret paper work to be mailed to Washington, and the return load is used top-secret paperwork to be shredded."

Grinning like a little schoolgirl, she asked, "How do you do that?"

Returning the grin without knowing why, he asked, "Do what?"

"From a stop you go through four gears making a left or right turn."

"The first four gears break inertia and get you moving; the rest build up speed."

They were now on Interstate 15, bearing south, out of town. She could feel the warmth of their relationship grow as they talked back and forth. She spoke up, "I think I should tell you my chauffeur is part of my twenty-four-hour bodyguard service. They're not really there twenty-four hours a day every day, but they are there most of the time, and their job is to protect me from being kidnaped or whatever. I've never needed their services, but it scares me to think what could happen if they were not there. They don't interfere with my life, but stay in the background, aware of what's going on. I always let them know my plans, and what I'm doing. Does that bother you?"

"Absolutely not. Any time I can be of assistance to them, let me know, though I hope they never need any assistance."

They had gone around the mountain and were on the other side of Provo in open country.

"How's that air ride seat doing?"

"Great. I never sat on anything so comfortable."

"Would you like to drive?"

The smile left her face, and she looked worried. With no traffic in sight, he pulled off onto the side lane and came to a stop. She came around the doghouse, and he showed her the shifting pattern and how the two buttons worked on the gearshift. Then he let her sit in the seat.

"Don't be afraid of it. The size of the vehicle is what intimidates you. I'll be right here beside you, on the doghouse. First of all, you need to feel the difference in pressure between the clutch and the fuel pedal. With the transmission in neutral, let off the clutch and slowly give it a little fuel." He inhaled the relentless fragrance of her demanding scent, and whispered in her ear, "It's hard to be this close and not touch you."

She smiled and held on to the steering wheel with both hands while practicing on the clutch and fuel pedal. He regained his composure and announced, "Okay, were going to try going forward in gear and coming to a stop, so push the clutch in and hold it."

He released the brakes and put the gearshift in second. "Now, let off the clutch and press on the fuel pedal like you were doing. Remember, you have a loaded trailer behind you, and you have to give it enough fuel to pull it, but not an excessive amount. I'm right here behind you."

Slowly, she let off the clutch and pressed on the fuel. The tractor started lurching up and down in a straight, erratic motion. She screamed with fright and put her arms over her face. Shylo reached to pull down on the trailer brake lever, but was thrown back and forth like a cowboy on a bucking horse. The truck rolled to a stop. His voice started out as a yell, but ended as a soft whisper as she turned and threw both arms around him.

"Are you trying to kill us?" He stood there, holding her tight, and whispered in her ear, "I'm sorry I yelled at you. That will never happen again."

She had her right knee in the seat and her left foot on the floor. He was standing behind the seat, next to the doghouse. After a minute, she released her tight hold and leaned back to look in his soft brown eyes and say, "I'm sorry, it scared me."

Humbly, he stood there feeling the softness of her warm body. He whispered softly, "I love you."

She swallowed hard and closed her eyes slowly, while wrapping her lips and tongue around his. He held the back of her head with both hands while she ravished the back of his shirt with her fingernails. The momentum of the passion peaked, and gradually they separated and looked at each other. She whispered, "Maybe we should save some for later."

With despair, he whispered back, "Yes, later." For a moment they looked at each other and then he squeezed behind the seat so she could return to the passenger's side.

While one minute turned to the next, they talked to each other as they traveled. Her mother had been gone for so long that she had trouble remembering her, but the memory of her dad was still fresh in her mind. He was the family member that made their place of residence a true home.

Shylo said, "I've done this two-day layover in Vegas before, but the trouble is that I don't drink or gamble, and going to see the sights by yourself is not a whole lot of fun."

She smiled at him, and he smiled back. After a while, she ventured back to the sleeper and lay down. She fell asleep, and Shylo kept on traveling. A few hours later she woke up, slipped her boots back on and returned to the seat. "I didn't think I would be able to fall asleep with all the noise. Where are we?"

"Almost to St. George. There's a truck stop there we can eat at. Are you hungry?"

"My growling stomach is what woke me up."

"Good, the food isn't quiet like Renee's, but it tastes okay, and you don't have to worry about getting fat. Then, after we eat it will take about two hours to deliver the trailer and then a few minutes to go into Vegas." He glanced at her on the other side. "Have you ever eaten at a truck stop deli?"

"The first time you ever saw me I was in a truck stop deli eating."

CHAPTER TWO

Three hours later, the first shades of twilight covered the land. They had eaten, delivered the trailer and were checking into the penthouse at Caesar's Palace, which Jean had reserved. Shylo parked the truck while she had the luggage taken up to the room. He hurried and went up to the accommodations. He put his key in the lock and opened the door to find her waiting on the other side. She held her hands up in the air.

"See, I don't know about any other places, but this has got to be the best place here."

He walked up to her without looking at the room. "Any place you're at would be the best place here."

She moved even closer to him. "I think you're just prejudiced."

"I think I'm in love."

Slowly, she put her index finger under his chin and whispered in his face, "We have an enormously large shower."

Softly, her lips pressed against his, and his arms wrapped around her slender waist. Her arms went over and around his shoulders. The intimate sound of heavy breathing leveled off, while groping hands went unchecked. The passion of love led them to the king-sized bed, and a passionate sexual desire controlled their actions. Minutes later they lay under the sheet, out of breath. Slowly gasping for air, he said, "We never made it to the shower!"

"Later."

chapter three

Three days later they pulled out of Las Vegas with memories of an enjoyable time and a truck full of souvenirs. The world was better, and life seemed more like living for the both of them. They both smiled at the aspect of being together. They picked up the trailer at Ellis AFB and continued north toward home. Even with all the excitement and heart-throbbing moments, she knew it would feel great to get home.

"I'm glad we left before the heat set in. That way we already have the air conditioner on instead of having to start it up in a hot vehicle." The desired subject of her conversation wasn't the heat, but she had to have a place to get started, so she continued. "When do you think we'll get back?"

"About four this afternoon."

She looked at him intently and asked, "What are we going to do when we get back?"

He glanced at her one time, and needed no explanation of her meaning. After a moment of thought, he replied, "Right now we're going to take it one day at a time. It's only been a couple of weeks since you first captured my heart, and I want to see what you're going to do with it. But more important to you is the opportunity to get to know me. If we had an argument about something, and you know sooner or later we will, what's going to happen then? Let alone the fact that you're getting cheated. You have so much to offer, and I have nothing. You're going to have to come over and see the apartment I live in. It has all the mandatory lodging in one room, except for the bathroom. They graciously put that in a closet. And it doesn't really matter anyway, because the only thing there that's mine is my clothes."

She smiled and remarked in a matter-of-fact tone, "Good. When you leave there it will be easy!"

He glanced at her and smiled. "You're impossible, you know that?"

He looked at the open freeway, with no traffic, and asked, "You want to try driving again, or is that something you would just rather not do?"

"After what happened the first time, you sure got a lot of trust in me."

"Just because I let you drive my favorite truck doesn't mean I trust you."

"Give me a break!" She threw a wadded up piece of paper at him and then explained. "Actually, it's something I'd rather not do, but I hate to let Dustin get the best of me by saying he can do it and I can't."

"Well, he doesn't know you tried, and I won't tell him, but we will try again later when you feel more comfortable about it. Okay?"

"Yes. I just have two questions I would like to ask. You keep referring to the dog house. Where and what is the dog house?"

He grinned and apologized. "I'm sorry; I tend to take it for granted that everyone knows. You see this hump on the floor, between the two seats, and from the dashboard back? It fits over the motor. Mechanics have named the motor in a truck a dog, so consequently this hump has received the nickname 'dog house.'" He grinned and shook his head yes. "It's a good name; otherwise, it would have no name."

"That makes sense. Now, you refer to your truck as a twin screw. What's a twin screw?"

"Again, that one is another mechanical term that describes something. You see this toggle switch that says 'differential lock.' It locks the back drive axle in gear so that both rear axles are pushing the vehicle. The definition of twin screw is that it has two means of propulsion, such as two motors on a boat, two engines on a plane, or two axles on a truck."

"How do you remember all that information?"

He grinned and confessed, "It's easy when it captures your attention. There's no real intelligence to it; it just comes natural."

"I think it takes a genius to do what you do. Did you know my father was a genius?" He looked at her with a question in his eye as she continued. "When he was eighteen he was a radio technician in the Navy. When he got out, radios and movie theaters were popular, but the television didn't exist. He built the first TV set. He actually constructed and put together a transmitter to send the signals, and a receiver to pick the signals up and display the picture on a screen. He didn't think it was worth anything, so he failed to do anything with it. Everyone figured the radio was going to do away with the picture screen theater, and he just couldn't see what use his invention would ever have. So about a year later, a Mr. Farnsworth does the same thing—except he acquires a patent for his invention."

"Did he know your father?"

"No, they never met. He was a genius too, who had the insight to recognize what it might be worth. If my father had this insight he would probably have died twice as rich as he was. I realize it wouldn't have made him any better a person, but the truth is that he invented it first, and no one will ever know it. That doesn't really bother me, it's just an issue more than anything else."

He looked at her with a grin and asked, "Are you complaining or bragging?"

She looked back and smiled. "Neither one, I'm just talking about an issue."

chapter four

At five p.m. they pulled into the yard and stopped next to the office. Shylo looked at the windows of the building.

"Good, it looks like Troy is still there. I'll see if I can give him this paperwork before I spot the trailer, then I'll take you home."

"That sounds good. I'll have Renee fix us something to eat when we get there."

He heard the words she said as he was getting out. A few minutes later, he returned to spot the trailer and she asked, "Don't they have a fence around this yard?"

"You know, that's funny, they don't. This has got to be classified as one of the worst areas of the city, and they have an unsecured lot." He pointed at the east side toward the Union Pacific building. "That dirt road back there, hidden by the weeds, runs alongside the tracks and comes out on Second South."

He backed the trailer in along the side of the yard, dropped it and pulled the tractor out in the middle. He looked at her and asked, "I hope you don't mind riding in my three hundred dollar Rambler?"

"Of course not."

"Good. I'll get the car and we'll load the luggage in it."

They both climbed out, and she stretched while he went for the car.

He pulled up on the passenger's side, got out and opened the back door. She walked up and said, "Did you know that a tire on one of your duelies is flat back there?"

He grinned and shook his head. "Well, maybe I better have a look. I've never seen a duely." He walked to the back of the truck. "You're right, thank you. The outside tire on the right rear duel is flat. The first flat this truck has had. I'll get it fixed tomorrow.

Jean said, "Duel, duel, duel. I'll have to remember that one."

1977
Love gone wrong

CHaPTer one

Shylo lay very still in his sleeper, listening to the sounds of a late Missouri night.

The month of July was almost spent, and the air was hot and clammy compared to the cool, dry nights of the Rocky Mountains. Both the driver's and passenger's window were rolled down, but with no breeze the air contained the repulsive odor of a very old, unclean truck stop. The smell of diesel mixed with the scent of rotting garbage was the answer to his question earlier when he walked out of the twenty-four-hour cafe.

"I wonder why there's no other trucks parked here for the night. Their food is good." Now he knew why, but it was too late to find another spot to park. Finding a place to park a semi for the night could be a real chore at times, especially in unknown country. He was about a hundred miles west of St. Louis, Missouri. His trailer was loaded with salt products, everything from table salt to large blocks of animal salt, bound for the distributor in Columbus, Ohio. There was a guaranteed return load of building textiles waiting in Chillicothe, Ohio. He would deliver the salt first, pick up the textiles next, and then drop down to Louisville, Kentucky, to spend two days at his parents' house. It had been over two years since he had seen them, and they still hadn't seen his new truck. With the memory of all the traveling he and Jim had done in a truck that didn't even have a sleeper, he couldn't wait to show this one to him. The only trouble was that the hidden truth was, back then, every trip was an exotic adventure on the high plains. Today, even with a vehicle like this, the high plains adventures had turned into just plain old work. Even so, he was still proud of his cab-over Aerodyne.

It wasn't as big as the Aerodyne he had seen with Jim at the International Harvest show in San Francisco, California. That one had the king cab that actually had a king-sized bed in the sleeper and a door on the passenger side that gave access to the sleeper area. His was the standard cab with a double mattress in the sleeper and about half the area between the sleeper and the front, with no side door access.

He lay there flat on his back, still wearing his clothes from the day, and looking at the stars through the two small windows in the ceiling. He was tired when he lay down, but still wasn't able to find sleep because Jean was on his mind. It had gotten to the point that Jean was always on his mind; even when his full attention was on the front door, she was knocking at the back door. They had only known each other for a month, but all his waking hours included her, even when she wasn't there. Her face, her long blond hair and the lines in her body were a blueprint that was etched in his mind, and he kept going over the blueprint. He thought, *I needed this trip home so I can talk to Mom. She can tell me what to do.*

Suddenly the quiet stillness was broken. The door on the passenger's side popped open. Slowly, the figure of a person gently came in. For a moment he stood there studying the moonlit surroundings. Then he proceeded to search the glove box and top of the dashboard. Shylo reached for the gun that was in the dwell next to the bed. The intruder turned and came behind the seat. Shylo turned the light on in the sleeper.

Pointing the gun at the advisory, he asked as he sat up, "Can I help you?"

The guy jumped with shock at the lights coming on. For a moment it looked like he considered using whatever was in his right hand, hanging at his side. Shylo yelled in a loud, gruff voice and held the gun up higher.

"FREEZE, or I'll shoot!" The guy stood motionless, and Shylo persisted. "What are you doing here?"

"I thought the truck was empty."

Carefully, Shylo commanded him, "Put whatever is in your right hand on the floor!" He placed a butter knife on the floor. Shylo looked twice, and twice he said, "A butter knife! A butter knife!"

Slowly, he started to break out laughing. "What are you going to do? Spread me to death?"

The young man answered with a serious tone, "The edge on that thing will cut steaks!"

As fast as the laughter started, it stopped, while Shylo studied the rigid cutting edge of the silver knife. He looked closely at the invader, who appeared more in his teenage years than his adult years.

"What are you looking for?"

He stammered and dropped his head. "Anything of value, preferably cash."

"Why?" Shylo asked.

"I don't know."

"Why aren't you at home in bed?"

"I don't have a home, and I don't have a bed!"

He lowered the gun, but didn't take his eyes off the young man. He took twenty dollars out of his pocket and handed it to him. With a startled, questioning look, he looked at the money and then at Shylo.

"Well, take it and get out of here."

Confused, but quickly as he could, he latched onto the money and exited the way he came in.

For a moment Shylo looked at the knife, still on the floor. Then, with a smirk on his face, he pointed the gun at the passenger window and pulled the trigger. A steady squirt of water came from the gun and went out the window. He put it back in the dwell, turned off the light and laid back down.

CHaPTer TWO

The next morning, Joyce Desmond stepped outside her front screen door to retrieve the morning paper. For a moment she stood there with her mouth open, holding the paper. A large, bright red truck with a silver trailer was parked in front of her house. Even though she had never seen it before, she knew who was in it. Barefooted and in a night robe, she walked up to the side and knocked on the shiny red door.

"Mom."

She swung around to see Shylo standing at the front corner of the truck. First there was a quick squeal and a reaction like she saw a spider, then she ran and threw her arms around him.

"I love you, Mom! I heard you open the door."

"Shylo! Shylo! I didn't think I would ever see you again." For a moment they just hugged each other, and then she let go. Smiling from ear to ear, she said, "We have a surprise—guess what it is!"

"Well, judging from those Tennessee plates in the driveway, I'll bet Cannon is here."

"That's right, he and Sheila and their little three-year-old daughter, Vicky. She is absolutely the cutest little thing you have ever seen in your life. Let's go have some coffee. Everyone is still asleep, but we're gonna have fried chicken, milk gravy, bacon, rolls and eggs for breakfast."

Still grinning, he admitted, "I had to drive all the way home to get a good meal. Is Dad home?"

"No, but he'll be here tonight."

They eased back through the noisy screen door. A voice in the living room startled them. "You're just as ugly as the last time I saw you!"

He looked to see Cannon in a pair of green military pants, flip flops and a white tank top, leaning on a bookcase.

Shylo replied, "Listen to who's talking. Doesn't the government have enough money to buy you some decent clothes?"

He walked over, and Cannon stuck out his hand. Shylo slapped his hand out of the way and hugged his brother. They went into the kitchen and sat at the table while Joyce poured the coffee.

Shylo asked Cannon, "What are you doing up so early?"

"Are you kidding? By this time I've already processed three machine guns and put in a requisition for the bullets."

"Don't the bullets come with the gun?"

Cannon laughed and replied, "No, no, they're like batteries—you gotta buy them extra! So, enough about me. What's this I hear about you buying a truck?"

"Well, what did you hear?"

"That Santa Claus brought you what you always wanted for Christmas."

"Two blonds and a red head? No, but I did get a big red truck. Whoa, let's back up here. What kind of helicopter are you flying?"

"I've been training to fly the new Cobra."

"What kind of helicopter is that?"

"Well, if you took a go-cart and mounted a propeller on top, a rotor in back and then attached multiple guns and missiles to it, you would have a Cobra."

"I wouldn't think you could attach that much to a go-cart."

"The idea is for a Baby Huey helicopter to go out and find a parked convoy. He orders up three Cobras to start firing, and I tell you what, to watch three Cobras dump their load in the middle of the night you would swear the sun was coming up."

A little three-year-old girl, half awake and still in her pajamas, came in the kitchen and stood next to Cannon, looking at Shylo. He spoke to her, "Well, good morning there, beautiful. Are there anymore beautiful girls around here?"

"Yeah, my mommy. You look and sound just like my daddy."

"My name is Shylo; I'm your daddy's brother."

"My name is Vicky."

Cannon asked as he picked her up, "What are you doing out of bed without your mother?"

"She said to go and meet my uncle. Is Shylo my uncle?"

"Yes."

"How come he's your brother but he's my uncle?"

"That's just the way things are, honey. Your mommy is my wife. Did you know that?" She shook her head yes. "Well, if he's my brother, he's your uncle."

"Oh, okay."

He stood and picked her up in his arms. "Let's go see Mommy and get dressed."

CHAPTER THREE

Jean slowly browsed through each page of the paper while she ate her morning breakfast. Renee filled up her coffee cup and she asked, "Do you think they will really impeach President Nixon because of Watergate?"

"I wouldn't know, ma'am, but they sure are serious about it."

"It will surprise me if they actually do it, but like you said, they sure are serious about it."

She grinned and shook her head as she turned the page. "Appalling, simply appalling. Oh, will you tell Andrew that I'm going to need the car today? I need to go to Vernon Securities, and I think I'll go shopping afterward. I need a new dress for my birthday party. Tell him I'll be ready in about an hour." On August the fifth, Jean was going to be twenty-eight years old.

She went to her bedroom and picked out the clothes she would wear: a turquoise green silk blouse, with a matching knee-length skirt; black patent leather high heels, with a matching purse; and a black bra. She also added a dark pair of new panty hose. She put the clothes over her arm and looked at the crowded racks of clothes in her already remodeled walk-in closet and thought, *Oh well, what's a girl to do?*

She went into one of the guest bedrooms to get ready. She had been sleeping in the guest room because her bathroom was being remodeled and would still be out for a couple of days. It would be done before her birthday; she was having an enormously large shower installed.

An hour and a half later the long limousine pulled into the private parking of the Saltair building in the middle of town.

Andrew opened the door for her to get out and then opened all the doors for her as she entered the building and got into the elevator. They went all the way up and exited on the tenth floor. They stepped out facing the name "Vernon Securities," turned to the right and walked to the receptionist behind a half-moon counter. Mary watched them get off the elevator and went around the front of the counter to wait their arrival.

"Miss Rasmusen, I've been waiting for you. How are you today?"

Before Jean could answer, Jeffery Domain, the company president, greeted her. He ran her company, but Ron, her lawyer stepbrother, was Jeff's overseer.

"Jean, Jean, Jean, it's a real pleasure to see such a beautiful woman." He grabbed her hand and kissed it.

"Jeff, you're a womanizer, you know that." She was smiling and holding her hand out until he was through. "But I don't care. At least you know how to treat a lady."

He moved aside and held his hand out toward his office. "Shall we adjourn to my office?" But she was already headed in that direction. He looked at Mary and said, "Hold my calls," then he followed Jean.

Andrew took a seat in the lobby, where he always waited for Jean. Jeff followed Jean with a large smile.

He stepped in front of her and pulled his chair back for her to sit in, but she replied, "Let's just sit at the conference table like usual."

She sat at the corner, and he hurried to push her chair in.

"Can I get you something to drink?"

"A glass of water would be good."

He turned and went behind a bar, and in a matter of seconds he returned with a glass of ice water and a coaster.

She asked, "Where's Derrick? Would you mind calling his office to find out?"

Before he could make the call, Derrick came in and went to the table. He kissed her on the cheek and asked, "How's my favorite step sister?"

"Your only stepsister is doing great!"

He took his briefcase and sat across from Jean. Jeff brought some paperwork from his desk and sat at the end of the table. Ron asked, "What's this I hear about a man in your life?"

"What did you hear?"

"Well, just to hear about a man in your life is news."

"Yes, well, I'm sure I don't have to tell you anything, because you probably know more than I do. But, if you come to my birthday party on the fifth at my place you'll get to meet him."

Derrick grinned and replied, "I'm looking forward to it." A brief moment went by, and he continued, "Now let's get down to why we are here. I got back yesterday from Vernon Ships in Napoli, Italy. The property acquisition is all set up for enlarging the shipbuilding plant. The construction is ready to go, and it's my personal opinion that this is a major plus for all parties concerned. We all know that the business is definitely there, and we need to enlarge the facilities to handle the demand for this product. This move is going to double our size and not only make us capable of handling the demand for our product, but inevitably we will put out a better product. Santo Mario, the master builder at Vernon Ships, is absolutely happy with this step. Of course, he'll have to double his own workforce of seven laborers, but they won't be turning business away. When the project is completed in a few months, the existing place will build the yachts for our stores in the Grand Cayman and in Hollywood, Florida. The new section will handle our newest account for the Italian Coast Guard, and the recent demand for fishing boats for private enterprise. The only thing I can see in the near future is that the new section is going to need its own master builder to take care of the problems that will be so different from those specializing in yachts. But I already talked to Mario about this, and he said he would be willing to train someone if they were willing to take responsibility for that part of the workload."

Jean spoke up and said, "Maybe in the near future we need to look at putting a store in Napoli to handle the sales of our new business."

Derrick replied, "I don't think so, for a number of reasons. The Coast Guard really doesn't need to be sold on something that is already spelled out on a contract. The contract takes place of the store, and the lack of this added expense makes it easier to compete for this business. The fishing boats are a similar process, without a contract for more than one. And the different specifications for each boat make it easier to build without a middleman. The fishing boats are more critical than the yachts."

Jeff said, "My dealing with Santo in the past has always proven him to be a just, responsible person. If he is going to help train a person, then maybe he knows of one or has such a candidate working for him already. After all, it's not like they have master shipbuilders growing on trees."

Derrick pointed his finger at him. "You're right, I already spoke to him about this, and he does have such a candidate already working for him." He set his briefcase on the table and opened it. "Now, then, I have the paperwork here for the contractors and the property. And I'm sure Jeff has the paperwork for the money."

Derrick handed Jean his paperwork and added, "If I could get you to sign on the yellow highlighted lines and please ask questions." He looked at Jeff and asked, "If I could see your paper work." He took the papers and scanned through the legal jargon, highlighting the lines to be signed. Then he handed them to Jean and took the papers already signed. He stamped them with his notary seal.

After all the paper work was signed, Jean stood up and said, "Well, gentlemen, if that's all, I have a new dress to go buy!" They both stood up to excuse her, and she announced, "The first one of you to talk to Mario, tell him that a trip to see this new project would be a good excuse to go deep sea fishing."

Jeff watched her walk away. "Um, um…"

Derrick warned him, "Careful what you say there, that's my good stepsister."

CHapter Four

It was August fifth, and Shylo was hotfooting it for Salt Lake City. He was halfway between Greenriver and Rock Springs in Wyoming, and over three hours away from home. He was going to be late for Jean's birthday party, and he knew it, but there was nothing he could do about it. He thought about going to her place first, but Virginia Street in the avenues just wasn't a place you drove a semi to unless it was business. In all reality it would only take a few minutes longer to drop the unit off at the yard and take his car up there.

His thoughts kept returning back to his visit at his parents' house. It had been longer than he could remember since he had last seen Cannon and Sheila. He couldn't believe that his brother was going to fly the military's heavily armed Cobra. One thing for sure, he would make a good pilot, because if there was one thing he wasn't, that was trigger-happy. He was glad that Cannon seemed to have found his niche in life. He got the opportunity and had that long talk with his mother. He told her about his new love for a girl, and his mother kept smiling. But when he said the girl was different, she quit smiling and her eyebrows went up. Then he said that she was rich, and the smile slowly returned and the eyebrows went down.

She replied, "You just keep doing things the way you're doing them, one day at a time, and I guarantee you that one way or another things will work out." His mother always had the right answer, and he enjoyed counseling with her.

Then he took everyone for a ride in his new truck. Dad sat in the passenger's seat, grinning from ear to ear, while the others sat in the sleeper for a Sunday drive in the middle of the week. What he didn't know was that he was grinning from ear to ear too. Bonding with everyone made the visit great and memorable.

Mom had even given him a handpainted, antique china bowl and platter to give to Jean. Since he didn't have a birthday present, or the time to go shopping for one, he hoped that the gift from Joyce would suffice. He felt guilty that he hadn't taken the time to go buy her something, but he knew it would be impossible to shop for the person who has everything. Thanks to the goodness of his mother, he wouldn't be going empty-handed. His mother was like that; she knew what was needed without being told.

It was already dark when he pulled into Beehive's yard. He grabbed his suitcase and shaving kit and birthday present and locked the truck.

Driving his Rambler up to the Federal Heights area, where Jean's estate was, he pulled up to the gate that had been left open for guests and decided not to try and park in the crowded driveway. He would park out on the street—preferably far enough away, where no one could see his vehicle. Then he looked at what he was wearing, a brown short-sleeved shirt and dark blue polyester bellbottom pants, but it was already ten p.m.

"Oh well, I'll just have to stay in the background. I could help the servants, but even they are dressed better than I am."

CHAPTER FIVE

In the large room with the vaulted ceiling, the glow of soft lights enhanced a pleasant atmosphere, while a jazz band produced a short range of gentle sounds. Eight couples of the fifty people danced cheek to cheek in front of the band on the south side of the room. Everyone else was either sitting at private tables, watching or mingling between the bar and the banquet table on the north side. George Jones, dressed in appropriate cowboy attire, stood at the bar, looking at Jean. He commented to Renee, who was tending bar, "I've never seen anyone drink beer from a brandy snifter." He continued looking at Jean and grinned.

"I guess if you're that rich you can drink it from the toilet if you want."

Renee straightened his shoulders and spoke as George turned to look at him.

"You know, I do recall her saying one time that she thought beer was human piss."

He looked at George's empty glass, raised his eyebrows and asked, "Would you care for another glass of draft, sir?"

The large grin left George's face. "No."

All evening, Jean had been drinking beer from a brandy snifter. For a person who hardly ever drank, the alcohol spirit was overtaking her without her knowledge. She wore a bold, strapless, ivory colored evening gown. The large Southern ringlets of golden hair were beginning to fall out and give her an even more desirable appearance. The clear Cinderella high heels had already come off, because she found them impossible to stand in without stumbling. Without being challenged, she told Miss Petty, "It's my place, I'll take my shoes off if I want!"

Not knowing if he should ring the doorbell or just boldly walk in, Shylo stood there, looking at the outside of the door. Then, without warning, the door opened quickly, causing him to jump back. An older couple stepped out, dressed to attend the king's ball.

She was wearing an evening gown with appropriate jewelry. His attire was a tuxedo with bow-tie and tails and black patent leather shoes.

The older gentleman said, "Hi, sorry we have to go, but we have a full day tomorrow. Goodbye." Before Shylo could say anything, they walked around him and left.

With the door open, he walked in through the receiving hall and into the large main room. He placed his gift on a table that was adorned with many wrapped presents. He sat a large gift on top of his unwrapped bowl and platter and turned around to see if he could see the birthday queen. She was leaning against the end of the bar, with her eyes on him. He observed the harmony and worth of her delicious beauty. Truly, she needed a diamond crown to top her head. Leaning against something and not talking hid her true condition from him. He walked over to greet the one he loved.

Just before getting there, he stopped when she said, "Well, well, well! If it isn't Mr. Cool in person! Taking the time to make a personal appearance!"

He stopped and lifted his head at the adverse sound of her words.

George Jones stood up from his bar stool and asked, "Would you like me to see him out?"

Without taking her eyes off Shylo, she said again, "That wouldn't be very hard!" Her speech was uneven and slurred. "You know why?" His eyes clouded as he listened to her talk. Everyone not dancing was looking; those dancing had stopped to see what everyone was looking at, and with a domino effect, the band had stopped playing to look. With a straight look and a wavering head, she answered her own question.

"He doesn't have the guts to stand up for himself!" He dropped his head, making no sound while she continued. "He'd just run; I got to admit, though, he figured out how to run and get paid for it!"

He turned and started walking back to the door.

She stopped leaning against the bar as her voice slowly raised to a scream. 'That's right, run, you coward. RUN! I HATE YOU! I HATE YOU!"

With her tongue over her upper lip, and the posture of a true female, she reared back and threw the brandy glass at him. It hit him square in the back and burst, sending glass and beer everywhere.

He stopped for a moment, with a beer-soaked shirt, then continued out of the room when she screamed again, "I HATE YOU!"

With her lower lip quivering as she watched him exit, she put her now sobbing face in her hands and spoke more normally, "Oh, God, I love him!"

Moving closer, George put his arm around her. She made a fist and punched him in the face. Caught by surprise, the force of the blow caused him to waver back. With a strong right forelimb, he backhanded her, knocking her to the floor.

From out of the shadows, Andrew, her bodyguard, was standing in front of George. With a sharp blow from the back of each hand, George was sent to the floor. He stood back up to rush him, but with the grace and poise of a ballerina, Andrew performed a three hundred and sixty degree spin, raising his right foot to his opponent's face, sending George back down. He could have knocked him out, but he wanted to look in his eyes and make sure he got the message, so his kick was measured with just such force.

For a moment he lay on the floor, facing the opposite direction, and once again he attempted to rush him. Once again, Andrew did a three hundred and sixty degree spin, except this time he grabbed George's right hand and twisted it as he turned. With the entire arm being held straight under this stronghold, Andrew kicked the elbow hard enough to bend it backwards. A scream of sheer pain broke the airwaves as George fell to the floor.

Holding his injured limb, he yelled, "YOU BROKE MY ARM! YOU BROKE MY ARM!"

Andrew grabbed the hair of his head, slammed it on the floor and said, "You ever hit her again and I'll break your neck!" With his nose touching George's, he asked, "Do you understand?"

George's eyes were so big he looked like Marty Feldman. Andrew answered, "Yes, I believe you do!" He let go of the hair, and George's head dropped on the floor. His face winced from pain. Andrew stood up, walked over to Renee and asked, "Did you call an ambulance?"

"Actually, I called the police and reported that someone had attacked Jean. When you stepped between them, he attacked you. Anyway, they'll be here any minute and they can access what needs to be done."

Andrew grinned at Renee. "You're a smart old man, you know that?"

Miss Petty helped Jean to her room and proceeded to take care of her. Almost everyone was gone by the time the police got there. They called an ambulance for George, wrote down Renee's statement and left.

Jean lay across her bed and slept until after noon the next day, without the knowledge of time or reason. When she woke up, she was still in her evening gown and suffering her first hangover. The memory of what she had done to Shylo slowly made its way back into her self-known truth. She had rebelled against his independent lifestyle, but the idea was not to drive him away but to change things for the better without being dominating. If they were going to be together, then he couldn't be running all over the countryside without her. She held her head and wondered how things got so messed up, and how long she had slept. It felt like it had been days.

Shylo went to his one-room apartment where he could lay in bed and figure out what had happened, or why it had happened. Trouble was, when he lay down and shut his eyes, his brain turned off.

Early the next morning he left to turn in his paperwork and pull his tractor out from under the trailer so it could be delivered. During his short drive to Beehive's yard, he went over everything that had happened the night before. Deep in his heart he knew what the problem was: Jean didn't want to be a part-time girlfriend during his short stays at home. She wanted to be a full-time, hello-every-morning-and-goodnight-every-night sweetheart. For years he watched this circle of disharmony take place between his mother and father, and now, in effect, it was happening to him. But maybe this wasn't the case. Maybe, after a few short weeks, she wanted to get rid of him but had to get drunk to say so.

This thought probed his mind as he stood at the counter and listened to his boss without actually hearing him. Troy snapped his fingers twice in front of him to gain his attention.

"Earth to Shylo! Earth to Shylo!"

Shylo shook his head and replied, "What?"

"Did you hear anything I said?"

"No."

"Then let me repeat myself. I need you."

Shylo backed away from the counter. "But I'm not that kind of a boy."

Troy grinned and continued talking. "I got a refer trailer in the yard loaded with military supplies from Tooele, for Fort Bragg, California. It should have left here yesterday, but John's truck broke down and everyone else is obligated. I've been desperate for a driver!"

Shylo looked at Troy and asked, "Why do you have military issue in a thermo unit?"

"Because the return load is fish guts."

Troy stood there grinning at the sight of Shylo's dismay. "It's not as bad as it sounds. After Fort Bragg you'll drop down into San Francisco and pick this load up. The guts are frozen solid and wrapped in plastic on skids that are approximately six feet tall. Set the thermo unit on zero and the load will stay frozen. Just make sure you start it at Fort Bragg so you can see if it's going to work okay."

For a moment, Shylo remained looking at him with his mouth open. Finally, he asked, "Where is this load going to?"

Troy laughed. "Oh, uh, the fertilizer plant in Ogden."

chapter six

Jean sat on the deck over the garage. With her feet on the rail, she leaned back in her chair while looking over the vast Salt Lake Valley. Three days now into her twenty-seventh year and not a word from Shylo. She feared that maybe she would never hear from him again. After what had happened, she couldn't blame him if he never spoke to her again.

Renee showed up beside her; it was one p.m, and he was carrying a large silver tray with her lunch. He set the tray on a small table and then put the table beside her chair. He stood there awaiting her word. She looked up at him.

"Thank you very much, Renee. You're way too good to me."

He remained standing there for a moment and then asked, "Can I get you anything else?"

"No, this is more than enough." She picked up the cup of tomato soup and took a drink. Renee turned and left. She wasn't really hungry, but because he had fixed it for her, she intended to eat.

Looking back over the valley, her thoughts returned to Shylo. She had to get hold of him and talk. If they could just sit down together and talk rationally, they could work things out.

At the same time that she was thinking this, Shylo was thirty miles away from the Golden Gate Bridge. He was hotfooting it to get into the city and find the bayside company "Fish Processors, Inc." so he could get loaded and underway before the day ended. The refer trailer was one of three used ones that Troy had purchased. Beehive Transfer had the rights to haul perishables, and Troy planned to use them.

His remark was, "It's worth getting into that business to stay in business."

This was the first time one of the trailers had been used. Shylo had started the thermo unit before leaving Fort Bragg. It took a while before the green light came on, but it seemed to be working okay. The green light switched to yellow more often at that low a setting, but even when the yellow light was on it meant that the Thermo King was working to bring the temperature to zero.

The sight of the Pacific Ocean was dynamic, and he had stayed on the highway for little less than two hundred miles to enjoy the scenery. The narrow single lane on each side was a challenge to drive, but God's scenic exhibit of the contrast between land and water gave him a peace of mind to evaluate what he was thinking about. He knew that he had to see her once more. If he could talk to her in a calm atmosphere, then he would be able to tell if she really wanted him or if he should shake her hand and say goodbye. That would be a hard act to perform, but if she really didn't want him, he would have to stage it.

He put a hold on his thoughts as he entered the pavement of the Golden Gate Bridge. It didn't matter how many times he went over this bridge, the awesome structure of this manmade marvel always captured his attention. The tollbooths were still a ways ahead, and the traffic seemed lighter than normal, so the precedence of the moment was to keep on trucking.

Then, without warning, and at an unbelievable speed, a tire came crashing through the center of the windshield.

Jim Sheffield, a long-time resident of San Francisco, was sitting down to dinner with his family and visiting parents. Jim had been promoting this event for many years, and the day had finally arrived when he and his wife and three-year-old daughter and four-year-old son were going to eat and socialize with his mother and father. Five years ago, Jim got his girlfriend pregnant and had to marry her. His parents did not agree with this. At the time he was a twenty-one-year-old hard worker, who would be successful in the construction business and didn't need his parents' permission for anything. Back then he told them that too, but it didn't take long for his ego to change, and he had been trying to turn things around since.

Everyone was seated around the table, looking at him. He bowed his head and gave thanks to God for all he had and the fellowship that was taking place. He ended his prayer by acknowledging Jesus Christ as his Lord and Savior. Everyone said amen and looked up. He looked up to see the east side of the Golden Gate Bridge through the room's large windows. He said, "Oh my God!"

A large semi was shooting over the side of the bridge. It was a red tractor pulling a silver trailer. The bottom of the fuel tanks had been crushed open by the large cement retaining wall, and the fuel was burning with a blaze of glory. Like a diver jumping from a cliff, the vehicle made a long, spectacular nosedive in the water, with the trailer pushing the tractor straight down.

1977
YOU BET

CHaPTer one

Slowly, Shylo opened his eyes and focused on the person next to his bed. "Did I go to heaven?"

Jean answered him with a question, "What makes you think you went to heaven?"

"I'm looking at an angel, so I must be in heaven." She grinned and shook her head no. He asked, "What happened?"

"What do you remember?"

"I was going across the Golden Gate Bridge, and this big black thing came flying in through the windshield. That's all I remember. Did I get hit by a meteor?"

"No, that big black thing was a tire and rim that came off a northbound car and bounced into your southbound windshield. Then you jumped the median, went over the top of a Chevrolet car and out the side of the bridge. Your truck hit the water and went under, and then came back up to float for about a minute and a half before it sank. During this ninety seconds an employee from a San Francisco tour boat jumped in the water and pulled you out of your truck. That was yesterday afternoon. It's now ten the next day, and this is the University of California Hospital in San Francisco. They said it was a good thing your trailer was empty, because that was why it floated for a little while until it filled up with water."

Looking like a person with a bad hangover, he tried to move. "I've got to make some phone calls."

She put her hand on his arm. "Whoa there! You don't have to call anyone. That's all been taken care of." He leaned back and looked at the IV in his arm. "Don't worry about that, it's just hospital procedure—anyone who comes in unconscious gets fed intravenously until they come to."

He looked at her with a serious question. "Did anyone get killed or hurt real bad?"

"No."

"How about the car I went over?"

"Well, either that guy has a guardian angel too, or your angel took care of him. He was released last night with some minor cuts and bruises."

"How did you get here?"

"I called your work yesterday to find you, and when I found out what happened I chartered a plane and flew in. After all, I have to take care of the man I love."

"After the last time I saw you, I was under a totally different impression."

She grinned back at him. "That was just a test."

"Well, did I pass?"

"Well, the test ain't over yet."

"I need to at least talk to my parents."

"I talked to them last night and let them know what happened. You can call them when you get ready, but first you need to see the doctor and get this IV out of your arm."

She leaned over and kissed him lightly on the lips. Then she whispered in his ear, "We'll save some for later."

CHapter two

Seven days later, after everything had been taken care of and he received a clean bill of health from the doctor, Shylo found himself on the way to the airport with Jean for a spur-of-the-moment trip to Italy. He didn't remember saying yes to this trip, he just knew that he wouldn't have said no if he had been asked.

He looked at Jean and asked, "Do we fly direct into Italy?"

"No, we have a two- to six-hour layover in Spain, and then a connecting flight into Napoli, Italy. There a car will pick us up and take us to the Persian Hotel."

"Who will pick us up?"

"I don't know, but he'll be working for the hotel."

He looked at her and grinned. "Oh."

"Hey, don't worry. We're going to have the time of our lives. We'll—"

He looked deep into her blue eyes and said, "Anyplace with you is the time of my life."

They stopped talking while they kissed softly and briefly. Then she asked, "What was I saying?" Gently, he touched the rose red lips on her voluptuous face, and the tingle of a thrilling sensation caused them both to shut their eyes and swallow hard.

The limousine made a right turn off North Temple and passed the place where couples parked to watch the planes take off and land.

God did turn the pages, and three days later Shylo and Jean, being led by an interpreter, were shopping for clothes on the narrow streets of Napoli. Shylo looked at Jean as they entered a store.

"Well, what do I wear to go deep sea fishing?"

"A hat and whatever else feels comfortable."

"Well, my Levi's and linen shirt feel comfortable."

"Then all you need is a hat. But get a couple outfits to wear later. I remember doing this when Dad was alive. He said he was coming here to check out his shipbuilding company but, of course, there was always a crew ready to take us fishing on one of the new yachts. First of all he always took me shopping for new clothes. This is the best place in the world to find the latest fashions."

"What am I dressing for later?"

"Tonight we're going to a large open-air restaurant with some authentic Italian dancing. Then tomorrow we'll go see Vernon Ships, and they'll take us fishing on a new yacht." She thought about it for a moment and then spoke again.

"Let me explain it to you so you're not in the dark. I don't have to see or do anything at Vernon Ships. Jeff at Vernon Securities, in Salt Lake, handles the business with the approval of Ron, my stepbrother, and my lawyer. I own both companies straight out. This is only the second time I've been here since dad died, and I'm anxious to see it. We are doubling its size and going from seven to fourteen employees. And if it warrants in the future, we plan to increase on that. So all we're going to do is look, okay?"

Shylo picked up a lavender blue silk shirt. "I'm really going to feel out of place there."

"Believe me, all you have to do is bend over and they'll have their lips stuck out."

Shylo laughed, Jean laughed and the young interpreter laughed and pointed at the shirt. "Nice! Nice!" He moved his head up and down.

By the end of the day, Shylo had a new Italian outfit by Gucci, and Jean had a new pants outfit by Valentino and a new dress by Versace.

At the end of their shopping spree they took their packages back to the room and lay on the bed, too tired to be excited about what they bought.

Two hours later they were awake and getting ready to go out. It was the second week of August, and the atmosphere outside was in the nineties even in the evening

At six-thirty p.m. they walked into Primo's restaurant and were escorted to an open-air patio with tables and a dance floor. Shylo was wearing the lavender blue silk shirt with black silk pants. Jean's new dress was a provocative display of interesting colors. Her bright yellow blouse had an attached black vest, which was part of the dress. The three-quarter-length dress was red with large yellow ribbons around the center and the bottom. The shoes were red, open toe and Italian leather.

They were seated at an intimate table for two with a tablecloth reaching the floor. At the center stood a large freshly lit candle. He looked at her sitting across from him.

"I don't know if I'm going to be able to eat or not."

"Why?"

"Every time I look at you I lose my appetite."

She grinned and blushed at his heartfelt remark. She knew that he had an awkward way of putting words when he was trying to be polite, but these word's were neither awkward or polite, but the straightforward truth, and she only had to look in his eyes to perceive the physical sensation being transmitted by his heart. This caused her own heart to quicken, her bosom to lift, her blood to race and face to flush. For a moment they held hands across the table.

A young waiter, who placed two menus on the table and left, interrupted them. They were written in four languages: Italian, English, French and German. For a moment they looked through the colorful folders and then Jean remarked, "I remember the last time I ate here. I had this indescribable spaghetti and meatballs."

"What, do you have to order the meatballs extra?"

"Of course, this is the gourmet capital of Europe! Didn't you ever see *Lady and the Tramp*? Well, they filmed them eating right here at this very table."

"You're wrong; it was out back, behind the building. See how much smarter I am than you!"

She grinned and raised her eyebrows. "They must have moved the table. How am I supposed to keep track of all that trivia?"

The waiter returned, and Shylo pointed at the picture on the menu. "Two Spaghetti Supremos with meatballs."

Jean said, "Make that one spaghetti dinner; I'll have the lamb platter."

She paused and looked at Shylo, who was grinning at her with a wrinkled forehead. She held up her hands and explained, "Spaghetti makes me sleepy!"

The band started to play soft, gentle Italian music while the tables slowly became more populated. By the time twilight had arrived a group of dancers, all dressed in colorful costumes, had gathered in the center of the dance floor. The band started to play the *Tarantella*, one of the oldest songs of Italian folklore, and the group started to dance. They formed a circle and started to rotate clockwise. The music started out slow and then changed gears to become a little faster. The dancers quickly changed their direction to counterclockwise. After a few changes in the momentum and direction, they were dancing away from each other to keep from being run over. But everyone was enjoying the event. The dancers stopped for a few moments to catch their breath and then returned. This time they coaxed everyone watching to join them.

Jean was the first out on the floor, dragging Shylo behind her. He was apprehensive at first, but by the time everyone was dancing away from each other, he was laughing as hard as anyone.

The dance ended and everyone stood on the floor for a moment, out of breath. She looked for Shylo, but he was gone. Slowly, she walked back to the table, still looking for him. When she reached her chair, he showed up beside her.

Taking her hand he said, "Come with me." He led her back out to an empty floor. He took a small jewelry box from his pocket. With everyone watching, he got down on one knee and presented the ring to her. "Will you marry me?"

The smile left her face, and she became very sober. Her eyes flooded with tears, and she took the ring from the box and tried it on her ring finger. It was too small. She rubbed the tears from her eyes, and he replied, "I'll have it sized."

"Yes." She put her arms around his shoulders and kissed his lips.

Seventy people clapped as they witnessed this scene. Only a few of them understood English, but everyone understood what had just happened.

CHAPTER THREE

The next morning, after an early breakfast at the hotel, they took a taxicab to Vernon Ships and arrived at the front of a warehouse. The building was one hundred feet from the Mediterranean Sea, and boosted a billboard sign on its top with "VERNON SHIPS" printed on both sides. One side faced the sea, and the other side faced the land. The landscape was open from the building to the water, where a pier harbored seven boats of various size and types. A bulldozer was working laboriously on a stretch of land to the far side of the warehouse.

They went in the front door of the building. Santo was there immediately to greet them.

"Jean, my darling, you have grown twice as lovely as the last time I saw you." He held her before him and kissed both of her cheeks.

"Santo, it's so good to see you again." She hugged him and turned to Shylo. "This is my fiance, Shylo James Desmond."

"What is this? You plan to get a married and tell no one!" He grabbed Shylo's right hand and shook it venomously. "Mr. Desmond, welcome to our little happy family. My name is Santo Mario, but please just call me Santo."

Grinning from ear to ear, Shylo said, "Yes, sir."

Santo was a well-groomed Italian with a small mustache. He spoke English well, but with a heavy accent. If you put a small hat on his head and pointed shoes on his feet, he could pass for a professional artist.

With a smile on her face, Jean announced, "Actually, you're the first one to hear about our wedding plans!"

"Then I'm extremely honored; let me be the first one to congratulate you!"

He grabbed Shylo by the shoulders and, as Shylo was afraid would happen, he kissed Shylo on the cheek. Shylo stood there with a straight face, thanked him and looked at Jean. Smiling real big, she raised her eyebrows. He held a straight face for a moment and then broke out in a large smile.

Santo asked, "Are you going to get married in Italy? One of our castle weddings does truly make you feel like the king and the queen."

Jean answered, "No, we're going to get married at home, but we will send you an invitation."

Santo held his hands in the air. "I tried with much effort to make the place clean for you, but it's totally impossible to keep clean and work too." They looked at the scene in the warehouse. Two twenty-eight-foot boats set on moveable A-frames were almost finished. All other tables and machinery seemed to be centered on these two projects. All materials needed were neatly stacked in front of the boats.

Shylo grinned. "I expected to see a long, slanted kind of a chute that went down to the water so that when the ship was done an important person hits the bow with a bottle of champagne. The bottle breaks, getting glass and wine all over everything, and the boat slides down in the water."

Santo laughed and shook his head. "You watch too much of the TV. Those are big ships—we build little ships; nothing over forty-eight feet long. Basically, there are four categories of boats: A, B, C and D. A is for the high seas, B is for the open sea, C is for the coast, and D is for protected waters. The two boats we're doing now are category B for the Coast Guard. They will be finished in a little less than two weeks."

Jean said, "I was hoping to see a little heavier construction on the north side of the building."

"And the day after tomorrow you will; the foundation and pipes have been laid, and the bulldozer is doing the finish work around that. Then tomorrow the material will be brought in and finally, as it was told to me, Deanthony Construction is going to jump on it like ugly in a boot." Everyone laughed at the humor of this remark, and Santo was well pleased.

For the next hour he showed them the highlights of custom boat building, and took great pride at the knowledge of his skill. Finally, after he was interrupted the third time by an employee, Jean asked, "You said Ace would be here with a boat to take us fishing."

Ace Proctor was a contractor that Santo used to deliver category A yachts across the Mediterranean, through the Gibraltar Strait and over the Atlantic

Ocean to either the store at the Cayman Island or the one at Hollywood, Florida. This procedure did not include handling their smaller boats, because shipping them would not be profitable. But by doing what it takes to stay in business, the two stores learned to handle the smaller boats from other suppliers, who dealt in new and used boats alike. Vernon Ships in Italy dealt only in what they built. Ace had two men who worked for him, Adriano and Marcello. Ace was not considered the friendliest of people, but his job called for that kind of a personality. Santo replied to Jean, "He's out back with Adriano and Marcello. They slept in the yacht they're going to take you out in. If you're ready to go I'll make sure they're up and decent for you."

Shylo looked at Jean. "Sounds good to me."

"This is good; I'll be back in just a minute."

He left, and Jean turned to Shylo. "I don't trust Mr. Ace. He's got a six-inch scar down the right side of his face, and he acts like the bad guy in a Western movie. And I swear if he ever cracked a smile he would look like a turkey turned upside down. The only trouble is that I hate to base my opinion on a person's appearance."

"Well, it sounds like a pretty strong opinion to me."

"Just the same, I want you to keep an eye on him."

He grinned at her and shook his head. "Okay, how is it that he's the one taking us out?"

"Believe me, Santo is paying him. Santo would love nothing more than to take us himself, but you can see how busy he is. It wouldn't be fair to take him away from his work, and when I say Santo is paying him, I mean Vernon Ships is paying him. Even though I don't trust Ace, I'm not complaining about him. He takes our best ships across the Atlantic Ocean and delivers them. The guy has to know what he's doing."

A little while later, Santo was showing them onboard the luxury cruiser.

"This is our category A boat. It is self-contained, diesel powered, has sleeping bunks for eight, a galley, a bridge, a hundred square foot deck, plus the captain's quarters." He introduced them to the three men behind him. "This is Ace, Adriano and Marcello. I'm a gonna leave you now in their capable hands, but I'll see you when you return." He kissed Jean on the forehead, shook Shylo's hand and left.

They stood there looking at Ace. He could speak English but had a much heavier accent than Santo. Shylo put the ends of his thumbs together and used his hands to outline a frame of Ace's head.

"You know, you're right, of you look at the outline of the feathers."

Quickly Jean spoke without looking at him. "SHUTUP!"

Ace smiled even larger. "We gonna catch the trophy fish. I know best fishing spot on whole sea. We go now, yes?" He was shaking his head up and down. They grinned back and shook their heads up and down.

Adriano and Marcello stowed the portable ramp and untied the boat. Ace backed her out of the slot, and they were underway. The two men spoke almost no English but were good at pointing or pantomiming what they were trying to say.

After an hour of traveling north, with the land just in sight, Shylo and Jean were set up in seats at the back of the boat. Each was given a baited fishing pole that was cast out by Adriano and Marcello. Jean's line was let out half as far as Shylo's, and Ace slowed the boat to trolling speed. Twice Marcello spread his hands apart saying, "Swordfish, swordfish."

Five minutes later, Jean had a large something on the end of her line. It made one hostile showing above water and dived back under. It was a trophy-sized Swordfish with a blue reflection in the glistening sun, a treasure to have mounted and hung on the wall. Ace slowed the boat down, and her line went loose. The trophy treasure got away.

He stopped the boat while Marcello repaired her line, and Adriano brought out finger sandwiches, chips and drinks from the galley. Shylo said to Jean, "Well, I have to say that these guys seem to be very good hosts."

She agreed by shaking her head. Still eating, she pointed where the fish was and spoke, "Did you see the size of that sucker?"

Two hours later they were trolling the same area with no luck. When Ace was about to give up on that area, Shylo got a hit on his line. It wasn't as big as Jean's, but still worthy of mounting on a plaque and hanging on the wall. Ace slowed down slightly and tried to maintain a steady force on the line. Shylo reeled the line in steady and watched his less colorful swordfish diving in and out of the water. Jean brought her line in while Marcello and Adriano waited to snag the catch with hooks on wood poles and bring it up on the boat.

Then, the crackling of wood exploding disrupted the event. The boat was heaved above the water and came down, violently shattered into two pieces by a large protruding rock. The immediate premises disintegrated in the matter of a moment. While the moment existed, Jean took a quick look at the captain's face—he looked more surprised than anyone. Everyone was cast into the water to hit the protruding stone. Shylo surfaced, looking frantically for Jean. Marcello and Adriano swam by him in the direction of land. He screamed, "Where's Jean?" but neither one of the two men answered or even slowed up to look at him. Thankful that they had all put life jackets on before leaving the pier, he continued to call for Jean.

Looking in the direction the two men were swimming, he saw a section of the boat being demolished against the rocks that were behind the one that had split the boat in half. The crashing effect was like sticks of dynamite exploding. The up and down motion of the disrupted waves against the rocks was causing him to go up and down in the water, and this was taking the breath of life from his body. Then he bumped into that large, unforgiving rock. He turned his head to find it wasn't the rock, but Jean. She was trying to swim and lead him toward the land. He pulled her back.

"We have to go out and around these rocks. We'll be killed if we go that way." He looked in her eyes; she looked as scared as he felt.

They swam back out away from the obstacles of sure death. The water was calmer, and they were able to stay afloat without consuming so much nasty saltwater. They were both tired and emotionally spent, but knew they had to get to land. He kept an eye on her while they swam parallel along the rocks until the rough water leveled out. Then they swam into the land. For a long moment they collapsed on the shore, resting, and then sat up.

Jean asked, "What happened?"

"Apparently, we crashed on one of those big, wicked-looking rocks out there. I don't know what happened to the captain, but his two-man crew tried to swim in through those rocks. I don't think they realized they were there."

"What are we going to do?"

"Well, for a minute let's sit here and regain our common sense." He looked at her with a heavy face.

"You scared me. I thought I lost you."

She put her arms around the top of his shoulders and whispered in his ear, "I love you!"

After a few minutes they stood up and surveyed the area. She said, "I think I swallowed enough saltwater to float a boat." The entire area looked uninhabited. She asked, "Where are we?"

He grinned and replied, "Italy." She pushed his shoulder and grinned. He replied again, "Maybe if we walk up to that high ground over there we can see what's around us."

As they walked, they talked about what had happened. He spoke, "This was the captain's fault because he wasn't paying attention to how close we were to that reef, but I can't help but feel guilty because he was trying so hard to help me land that stupid fish. I think he paid the ultimate price for his mistake, though. When we first went under the water I don't think he ever came back up. And I have a bad feeling his two-man crew was crushed or beaten to death in those rocks. If we spot them and I can get to them, I'll go pull their bodies out before they get washed back out to sea."

Slowly, they made their way up the incline, choosing their steps because they had no shoes on. They couldn't remember when they came off, but somewhere in the water were two new pair of slip-on tennis shoes.

Jean said as she stepped in his footsteps, "A hundred pairs of shoes at home, and I am walking barefooted over sharp little rocks."

After twelve minutes they reached the top and surveyed the area. No boats could be seen on the water, and the only house visible looked three to five miles away. They could see wreckage from the boat washing up on shore on the opposite side of the reef, but no people.

He said, "I've got no intentions of leaving you alone."

"Thanks."

"And I don't know about you, but I've got no desire to try and walk barefooted clear to that house, which is probably empty. Let's go check out the wreckage. Maybe we can find something to start a fire and attract someone's attention."

A few minutes later they walked out to a more desirable sandy beach. Jean plopped down in the sand. "I can't take another step; my feet are shredded!"

Shylo turned and looked at the bottom of her feet. He shook his head and grinned. "No, honey, they aren't even scratched. Mine feel the same way, and look."

He bent his leg so she could see the bottom of his foot.

"Give me a break!" She inspected the bottom of her right foot with disbelief. Then, letting her foot go, she grinned and looked up. "I like that name; I haven't been called honey since daddy died."

He grinned and looked at her. "I like you." He turned his attention back to the beach. "It looks like one person walked out of the water." She stood up and looked as he continued to talk. "I'm no tracker, but that looks like one person's set of footprints, and they must be recent because the tide would have washed them away."

They followed the impressions to the water's edge, and he continued to analyze them. "Looks like after they got out of the water they turned to look back, and then turned and left. Funny thing is, the way those tracks go straight into the grass, they either saw something or knew where they were going."

She spoke her opinion. "Looks to me like they were headed for that old house we saw."

He pondered the subject further. "Trouble is, you can't see that house from here."

He grinned and looked at her. "The Lone Ranger and Tonto got nothing over on us."

She grinned and pushed his arm. "You're impossible! Here we are in a life-and-death situation, and you're making wisecracks about TV stars." She stopped grinning and pointed out in the water. "I hope that's not what it looks like!"

He looked in the direction she was pointing. "I hate to say this, but I think it is! I'll go pull him in."

She took off behind him for the water. "Oh no, you're not going to make me feel like a wimp. My clothes were starting to dry too."

About waist deep in the water, they each took the hand of the dead person and dragged the body up on shore. It was Ace. He was killed when the boat first went down.

She asked, "Is he going to be all right there?"

It crossed Shylo's mind to say something funny, but he couldn't. "No, actually, he's going to attract anything that crawls, but anywhere we put him he'll do that. For right now he's okay." He went through the front pockets on the body.

"I know I saw him smoke." He pulled out a silver lighter and tried to light it. The wick was too wet. Leaving it open, he placed it on a rock. "We'll let it dry out for a while." He looked back out at the water. "We got the footprints of one person, and the body of another. We still have one unaccounted for. If you want to gather some wood for a fire, I'll go look around that reef for the missing person."

"Okay, just don't do anything stupid or get so far away that I can't hear you yell."

Forty-five minutes later he showed up, soaking wet, to a blazing fire.

"No luck, and I'm glad. I hope they both made it, but the truth is, with all that debris, I could have stepped on a body and never known it. Let alone the places I couldn't get to."

He gathered some green branches and threw them on the fire.

She spoke in defiance, "What are you trying to do, put my fire out?"

"White man can't see fire signals, only smoke signals."

She laughed and then said, "Okay, okay, spare me the rest."

Before the smoke could get very far in the air, the Italian Coast Guard was at the shore.

CHAPTER FOUR

The following morning, Jean and Shylo sat in the hospital room, waiting for Santo to show up. Shylo shook his head and grinned, wearing the hospital's green pajamas.

"I can't wait for Santo to get here so we can talk to someone who can speak English."

"Well, I can't wait to get back into some decent clothes."

A little while later, Santo showed up. He hurried into the room, carrying some clothes. He hugged them both and apologized for what had happened.

Jean assured him, "It was definitely not your fault, and it wasn't ours either. It was just an accident. A very grievous one, but still just an accident;"

She took the clothes he was carrying and divided them with Shylo. "I'm sorry I'm so late, but they didn't want to let me in your room."

"But I called them this morning and let them know that you were coming."

"I know, but when I didn't have your key to get in, they changed their mind. After I convinced them it was an emergency, the manager let me in but followed me."

She looked up and asked, "How about the shoes?"

He hit his forehead with the palm of his hand. "Oh no, how can I go and be so stupid? I even remember you requesting the shoes."

She took her clothes and headed for the bathroom. "Well, this hospital will just have to fight me to get these paper slippers back!"

Shylo stepped behind a bed curtain, and a moment later they stepped out in their clothes.

Santo held his hands apart, saying to the both of them, "You look so much better now. I talked to Marcello this morning."

Shylo spoke, "So Marcello is alive?"

"Yes, didn't you know that?"

"No, that phone call to you and the hotel has been our only English conversation since before the Coast Guard picked us up."

"Then you don't really know what all has happened, do you? Well, let me explain to you all that I know. Marcello has been right here in this hospital. I talked to the Coast Guard earlier this morning, and they recovered Adriano's body out of those reefs. It took a helicoptor to do it. Those reefs have such a bad reputation that they call it Dead Man's Point. Anyway, Marcello said that after the accident they didn't know what had happened or really where they were at. They thought something had blown up, but they could make out where the land was, so they swam that way until it was too late. When he realized where they were, Adriano was gone, so he just tried to swim out of the reefs and then to shore. He's got a broken arm and looks like someone was beating on his head with a two-by-four. So when he got to shore, he knew his uncle's house was only a couple miles away. He was raised in that area and knew his only choice was to get help."

Jean asked, "Did Ace have anyone?"

"Nobody that I know of, but I'm a sure that somebody is gonna crawl out of the woodwork. But Adriano had a momma and a papa, and by no means is it gonna be easy to face them."

Jean took Santo's right hand into both her hands and said, "I know there's no way we can replace his life, but I will try to ease his parents' grief."

"Thank you, Miss Jean. You're just like your father. He was a very great man." When Jean got home she was going to send a registered check to Adriano's parents for a hundred thousand dollars, and one for fifty thousand to Marcello.

She grinned and said again, "If we could get you to take us back to the hotel we would be grateful. I think this is one fishing trip that we will never forget."

Shylo looked at her and said, "I think you're right."

CHAPTER FIVE

Three weeks later a wedding was in the early stages at Jean's estate in Salt Lake City, Utah. The main event room was cleaned to a high shine. The folding chairs were placed in rows to face a flower-covered arch that stood ten feet in the air. All of her servants were dressed and present for the event, but not to work, as the work was being done by other people. A white grand piano with gold trim was present to play the wedding theme, and a three-layer wedding cake was on a table on the patio. Next to this was a large gazebo with a dance floor and band. On the patio with the cake were thirty formal tables set up with a vase of wildflowers on each one.

Derrick and Mary and Dustin were present. Cannon and Sheila and Vicky were present, and Joyce and Jim were present. Jean had chartered a plane to bring them in and was scheduled to return them home that evening.

Joyce was in Jean's room, helping her to get dressed in a stunning strapless white wedding gown with white gloves that came up above the elbows. Joyce was trying to put on Jean's makeup at her large vanity. She wiped off her forehead with a tissue.

"If you don't quit sweating, this makeup is going to run all over everything."

"I'm sorry, I'm nervous."

Joyce grinned with excitement and tried to coax out of her where they were going on their honeymoon. "I think you should at least let me know what country you're going to be in."

"I'll give you a hint; we're not going over any ocean. So it wouldn't be hard to figure out that we're going to be in the United States. Oh, by the way, thank you for that lovely china bowl and platter you gave me for my birthday."

"You're welcome, it was my pleasure." With everything done, Joyce pinned a decorative jeweled tiara on the top of Jean's braided hair that had been put up to hold the crown. This went over the veil that went down her back and covered her face.

Joyce then led her to the event room, where everyone was waiting. The pianist played the wedding march, and Derrick walked in to give her away. The minister performing the service conducted an emotional, flawless ceremony and asked Jean if she would take Shylo to have and to hold, forsaking all others.

She said, "I do."

Then he asked Shylo if he would take Jean to have and to hold, forsaking all others.

He said, "You bet."

THE END

About the Author:

On May 16, 1947, Terry was born at the Kings Mary Hospital in Portsmouth, Virginia. His mother, Bessie Ann LeMaster, worked in a shipyard. His father, Clarence Ottis LeMaster, who had been a radio technician in the war, learned to drive a truck and then taught his son Terry.

Printed in the United States
45689LVS00005B/97-114

9 781424 101474